DATE DUE

BY THE LIGHT OF THE JUKEBOX

BY THE LIGHT
OF THE JUKEBOX

DEAN PASCHAL

Ontario Review Press ✦ Princeton, NJ

Ontario Review Press
9 Honey Brook Drive
Princeton, NJ 08540

Distributed by W. W. Norton & Co.
500 Fifth Avenue
New York, NY 10110

Library of Congress Cataloging-in-Publication Data

Paschal, Dean.
   By the light of the jukebox : stories / Dean Paschal.—1st ed.
      p. cm.
   Contents: By the light of the jukebox — Moriya — Death of a street
dog — L'annonciation — Sautéing the platygast — Python — Genesis
— The puppies.
   ISBN 0-86538-105-4 (alk. paper)
   I. Title

PS3616.A79 B9 2002
813'.6—dc21   2001058097

First Edition

"Sautéing the Platygast" was first published in *Boulevard* (Spring 2002);
"Moriya" in *Ontario Review* 56 (Spring/Summer 2002).

CONTENTS

BY THE LIGHT OF THE JUKEBOX

Good evening. I see you have noticed the woman behind the bar. She was very friendly to you, too, I saw, when you came in, extraordinarily friendly, I would say. Why do I use the word extraordinarily? Well, look at the drink that she made you. And in a tall glass, too. She won't do that for everyone. She pretends not to have the ingredients.

You have not been here before, I know. How? Well, I'm here all the time, and I've never seen you. But that is not *how* I know. I am judging entirely by her reactions to you. First, she told you a joke; I can't remember the last time I've heard her do that. Second, you were discussing—the two of you were discussing; pardon me, I haven't been deliberately eavesdropping—a film, the Humphrey Bogart film; and that woman discusses nothing ever, with anyone, though she is very bright indeed when she does it. I understand that film has been restored perfectly and the sound is digital now. I saw that film once, myself, the original one, I mean, but that was years ago. Actually, I'm not certain the scratches harmed it.

Congratulations, I say. But I should also say you've just made a big mistake. You've sat down on a stool which is in entirely the wrong place. She will ignore you completely now, I guarantee. She will stay down there, even though it's only the three of us in the place. The dog doesn't count, of course, though, in truth, she speaks to that dog more than to me.

I don't mean to imply by that that she speaks to the dog a lot.

I mean she doesn't speak to me at all.

Ah! Immediately I see it! You have to control a laugh! Or pretend to. Yet another drunk in a bar! Yet another drunk with his secrets! (What if my secret is that I'm sober?) I'm not; but I see that you think *I'm* the reason she won't come down here. You are jumping too quickly to the most obvious conclusion. You will get nowhere with this woman if you jump quickly to conclusions, obvious or otherwise. Anyway, your mistake, though "big" is minor, too, and completely rectifiable. All you have to do is move to another seat. That's absolutely all you have to do. I invite you not to do that though, at least for a few minutes. I invite you to continue sitting by me for the space of your one drink, your *tall* one, granted. You are obviously interested in this woman and I have a thing or two to tell you about her that might very well change your life.

We wait, now, together. (Are we both watching the same rising bubble in the same luminous tube?) Still you hesitate, visibly. Why? Is it *gossip* you are shying away from? You are a true gentleman, then. But rest assured; that's not my plan. Anyway, why would you accept so eagerly in a movie what you will not even consider in real life?

OK, then. Very good. After all, why not? What can it possibly hurt? One drink then, here, by the light of the jukebox. What? Oh, no thank you. That's very generous. No. The empty beer bottle isn't mine. I always drink margaritas here. *This* is mine. Almost ludicrous, right? No doubt, you thought it was water. I pay three times the price listed on the mirror. And this is my very own glass. The plate of salt on the counter is mine, too, virtually exclusively. Margaritas yes. Me, and who else? The well-known singer....

Yes indeed.

Actually, like that well-known singer, I once had a twin-engine seaplane.

Very generous of you, I say, and mean it. But again if I might be permitted to be very slightly rude to a person I have just met, it also could have been a trick to try to get her to come down here. I am not insulted by that. But I ask you, please, tell me: why should you *need* such a trick? It should happen naturally. It's not far. It's exactly twenty-two feet to where she is sitting now on the stool behind the bar. It should be the simplest thing in the world. It should happen naturally. It's actually rude for it *not* to happen. But it won't. It will not happen even if we both sit here till sunrise. Of course (as you seem to have guessed) you could always order another drink. I, too, could order another. I don't talk. *We* don't talk, as I've said. I order another drink simply by raising my empty glass. She would come then, and immediately. But that's cheating.

Let us not mince words. Let us move quickly. You are indulging me. So, I will tell you up front.

You are not the first man to think he's discovered her.

You are not the first man to ask himself—on hearing the heavy door of the bar shutting slowly, pneumatically, behind him—to ask himself, how can such a thing be? To not quite believe what he is seeing. There are scarcely three women of equal beauty in the entire town. I say three. That may be an exaggeration. Maybe there are three. There may *not* be. How can this be? What is going on here? How can it be so quiet? Only a few minutes away, every hag of a female bartender is perpetually surrounded by a noisy crowd of admirers. And here. There is no one. Not one person. And, look at her:

She condenses beauty out of the air.

Think about it. Patience. Trust me. It may be why you should listen.

We could first address why she is not coming down here. If I say it's not me. (And I do.) And I say it's not you. What other reason could there be? Could there be something, well, slightly odd, slightly unexpected. Could there possibly be some different quality to the *space* here?

Well, well, well. *Now* we're talking.

In truth, it is nothing I myself perceive. The light here is more colorful, perhaps. But then again, I don't have her eyes.

Look at them, though, more carefully. I won't say what color they are; you can notice that when you get closer. But what you may also notice is that you can describe her eyes without any reference to color at all. Her eyes are the moth's eyes with the glint of the flame in them. An interesting thing, though, about colors, not just eye-colors. As a child you need only a few: the brightest reds, greens, yellows and blues. Later, it's not so much that you need more, as that you don't need the bright ones any longer. You don't even *think* in those colors anymore. It is possible, you know, to follow the glint of the moth's eyes all the way to the flame. It takes practice, a lot of it. But it can be done. I suggest (at first, that is) a low-wattage bulb. If you practice long enough, you can not only see but *watch* them. Why do I say this? Well, once again, look at her eyes.

People (people that I know, that is) have come by here at three, four, five in the morning, attracted by the dim, moving light. The bar is closed then, of course. They have peeked though the curtains in these windows and sometimes seen her sitting there. Exactly there. Staring at the wall. Evidently that stare can go on for hours: two, three, four hours, till sunrise, evidently. At which time she might lie down and go to sleep on one of the couches.

They have told me these things. They have worried about her and mentioned it to me. Why? Because. Well, because we were an item once. I don't say this to scare you away. It is merely a fact, very well-known. That was long ago, though. That relationship, like so many others in life, is buried in a joint grave with a joint tombstone and a joint epitaph reading: "We might have been happy."

Like so many others, I say.

The juke box was brand-new then. The jukebox is not really an original. It's a replica of a classic style. Actually, if you notice, it plays compact discs. The truth is, I'm a bit suspicious of such things. It's like the film restoration that we mentioned earlier: Why can't we have our *own* past?

When the jukebox was shiny-new, a deaf couple would come in here almost nightly and dance to it. They felt the vibrations of the music, of course, as deaf people do, another well-known fact. It was interesting to me personally, though, to actually see it. But something else was far *more* interesting. They had a favorite song.

That's apropos of nothing, perhaps. But it long ago entered my mind so firmly that it might relate to my tale in a way that is not clear to me.

We met, this woman behind the bar and I, not so long before that. We met, actually, in another bar. It was inevitable, perhaps, as much as we both drank in that era. Indeed, it was because we liked to drink so much that she bought this place. I helped her fill out the papers for the license. The exact length of the bar had to be in the application. That's how I happen to know it. Drinking. Our entire lives revolved around it. The most energy and enthusiasm we had in each and every day was just before we started to drink again—usually (though not always) in the evening. I had some money then. Some time. Some women, too. More at first, then less. Some of the women became somewhat afraid of me—physically, I mean, more specifically sexually. They worried, perhaps, about my stability. Then I met her. She was not afraid.

Sex, you know. It's interesting, the theories; there are basically two. One is that any woman can, if she puts her mind to it, do absolutely anything—sexually, I mean. No limits. Most don't and won't and haven't and never will. But that's the theory of women and that theory remains completely unaltered in the face of abundant ... experience. An elegantly simple theory; yet entire cultures, the Moslem, for instance, seem to have lived in utter fear of it. On the other hand, the theory of men is messier, more complicated. God himself (or Allah) gets involved with the theory of men.

As you might have already guessed, we were into sex. We were into drinking. We were a complete "item" as I say. But years ago. The sex we shall speak of in a minute, though only briefly. That is not what I want to talk about just yet. I'm not quite finished with the space. We were talking of *space*, remember. Dimensions. Not anything astronomical.
Patience.
Allow me to describe this room to you. You are sitting in it the same as I. But allow me to describe it nevertheless. I may be in a somewhat different *space* than you. My perception of it may be different, I mean. You see only the woman that I am momentarily keeping you from. She is organizing this area for you. There is some excitement, some anticipation, some slight undercurrent of erotica perhaps. That is the atmosphere for you. She is all you are seeing. But I am not seeing her at all. What I am seeing is far more physical; some advertisements duct-taped to the mirror, three lamps such as would normally be in living rooms at the end of sofas—somewhat strange, actually, for a bar. Three…
But wait! Wait a minute! Look at her now; she is smoking—a prolonged gesture, cool, serene, that long straight arm, that perfectly white arm, that face, too; that face which has twice been in advertisements in national magazines. Am I kidding? Does it *look* like I'm kidding? Then the smoke once more, cool, grey, somewhat humidly vaporous in the light. She is ultimately a creature of smoke and sand. Why do I say ultimately? Why do I say sand? You'll see. She wipes the varnished, laminated wood, folds the bar-cloth, wipes it again. Notice, too, as I warned you, despite your talk and joke. (Didn't I warn you?) It's as though you don't exist.

Now, once more, and carefully, she is putting her cigarette down, the final thoughtful drag, then beginning to cut some more limes. (Those will be for me, incidentally. We don't speak but she looks after me. She will cut quite a lot of limes. No matter. They will all be for me. I shall drink them.) Everything about her motion is synchronous gesture, a steady ballet of endeavor, silently timed; such is life, or can be, for human-beings, against the elaborate belly-exposure of the other mammals. She makes you see it, though, makes you *aware*. That, too, is very important. She is left-handed, as you may have noticed. Watch. She will place the point of the knife, the very tip, into the lime to "pin" it, so to speak. Up close, you would see a tiny squirt of lime juice, then the lime itself, being pressed spheroidal, tense with fluid against the marble of the cutting board. Then, suddenly, completely in half! So quickly it takes your breath away! But perfectly silent, absolutely *without* a sound. How can she *do* that? That strong left hand. The point of that knife. The perfect and instantaneous reversal of the thrust.

Actually, she's into weapons, generally. There are knives all over her house. One, especially, I well remember, a short, curved one, which fits in a jeweled scabbard, like a small scimitar. It is of an Arabian style, of a specific type. I don't know whether you are a reader as well as a watcher of classic films, but Sir Richard Burton mentions the type in his *Book of the Sword*. An absolutely fascinating blade. The knife belonged originally to her great-great-grandmother, who evidently had it made. (Not her great-great-grand*father*, but mother, mind you, mother.) There is a specific name for it. Was her great-great-grandmother possibly Arabian, then? A dweller, possibly, in tents? I don't know. She has never said.

There is a problem with the knife, though. There are gargoyles engraved on the handle. I don't think the *gargoyle* is an Arabian symbol. So what would be the connection, then? A crusade? A modern crusade? A *more* modern crusade?

She always kept that knife in a cubbyhole at the head of her bed. For safety, security, she said. And I believed her. Strange, how the sharpness of that blade would enter your mind. Even with everything we did together in that bed, only twice, in all those years, did I forget entirely about that blade. And then only for a few seconds.

A woman with sharp knives, strong hands and perfect coordination; a perilous woman, you may already be imagining.

And, indeed, it can be a frightening thing to sleep with her.

You say nothing, look embarrassed, surprised, that I should I mention such a thing—sexually, you are thinking. The obvious thing, and I don't mean to insult you. Well, that, too, as I have already implied.

But I was thinking much more literally. It is frightening to have someone suddenly sit bolt-upright beside you in the bed, talking gibberish, and seeing things in the room. At such times, she may look absolutely through you. It may take a long time to wake her up. Quite a long time. You may have to talk her down. You may have some worries as to whether or not it will be possible this time.

A perfectly normal life may well be a thing done with mirrors. Many, if not most, species of *ab*normal life may represent a mere unsilvering of those same mirrors. If time is the agent, it won't happen all at once. My grandmother, for instance, became a "funny" woman before she died. She had been given a heavy sterling-silver hand-mirror as a teenager, on graduation from high school. She used that mirror exclusively all of her life. She was very old when I knew her. By that time, when you lifted the mirror it made a flaky sound inside. I tried to use it once to comb my hair. To my surprise, I found the task completely impossible. There was not enough image left in the glass to do that. Quite honestly, not even enough *image* to comb my hair.

That may be the norm. But that is not all that can happen in life. It is possible for *forces* to enter your life, and if they do they will be of a different urgency and intensity. They will tend not to wait around.

The sitting bolt-upright in bed, for instance, what was that all about? What could it have been that so scared her? One night I was there, when suddenly, I was awake, wide awake, we both were, in the dark. There was something in her closet, in the dark, in her bedroom; I heard it. She heard it. A rat? A cat? I thought of both possibilities. We were both awake, wide, wide awake. A rat or cat, I thought.

You would think that, too, sitting here. But the noise this thing was making was not the noise a rat or cat could make.

It was whispering, steadily whispering, minute after minute, whispering.

I tell you, I speak three languages and for the life of me, I could not understand a word. Or, then again, perhaps I *could*, which, in a way was even *more* frightening. What I was understanding though, what I understood, were only articles, such words, you remember, as *a*, *an*, or *the*. But scattered though several languages: *la, los, el, al, les, la, los*... A cat, a rat, a dumb animal, cannot consistently form words, even articles. (Why do I say consistently? I don't know. I'm being prudent, I think.)

There were no nouns or verbs that I could make out. No substance or action. But a whispering, still, a whispering. Fate itself might speak this way.

I was stirring around in the bed. Quite honestly, I was *not* starting to get out of it.

Don't! She said, Don't look! It will go away!

She was covered in sweat, her skin slick to the point of being slimy. But cold, too, gelatinous. We were holding onto each other for what they call dear life. Never once did we clinch in love or lust the way we clinched that night in fear.

I did not move. I did not open that door. *You* would not have moved or opened that door, either. You would not have budged from that bed. I did not. I told her to turn on the light. It was on the nightstand on her side of the bed. But she wouldn't and I wouldn't go myself, go around her, I mean. She was in tears in the moonlight. She seemed to be awake. She seemed to know what she was saying. Maybe she knew what *it* was saying. I don't know. Whatever she said, I would have believed. I would have believed anyone or anything that was telling me not to move from that bed or open that closet door Not long, all of this lasted, but it seemed long: five, six, seven minutes...

It was whispering. We were whispering, too, or I was.

Have you ever seen it? I said.

Hush! It will hear you!

(Tears she was crying. She was tremulous; sweaty also, but icy cold.)

Have you ever *seen* it?

Hush!

Through the parted curtains, I could see the moon outside. It was a perfect moon, perfectly round and clear, spectacularly clear and bright. It was such a moon as might appear above a desert sky.

Then it was gone. We turned on all the lights, but left the door to the closet closed. As impossible as it seems, we drifted off to sleep. We did not open the closet door till almost noon the next day. At that point (cautiously, though) I opened it myself. I saw nothing inside, almost literally nothing. Of interest that is. Some worn, mismatched shoes. Some rusty coat hangers, no two alike; her panties on the floor, some sand there, a bit of sand, some sheer black stockings, a man's tie, new-looking (not mine). No two of anything alike, it seemed. There was a hole in the floor, too, a section of the old floor missing. The bent coat hangers. That was it.

It was sobering, that moment, looking into that empty closet. It caused me to begin to reassess our lives. We were getting older. We had spent too much time in bars, too much time in bed with too many separate people. We had not so much to show for it, even the memories were vague. Most of the sweat in life should come from work, not sex. With us, it was not that way.

Looking down in the closet, it dawned on me, reliving the scene of the night before, that what she might have been experiencing was a sexual fear, a fear of that thing *mating* with her.

I did not mention this. I was simply looking around in the closet. For once in my life, I was having a moment to think. Interesting, when one is living a purely physical life how critical one becomes of purely physical things. Of *her*, for instance. She didn't look to me, then, the way she looks now. Actually, in that era, I thought she was a bit fat. I thought she had no legs. I thought her hands were too rough and scarred, too grasping, too, well, whatever... obviously *funct*ional, perhaps. But look at them now. Would you please look at each and every thing I was once criticizing. Very strange, what has happened to her. I do not believe I could have been so completely wrong. I believe she may have changed over time or *be* changing. She may be coming into focus.

But then, that day, standing before the empty closet I poked around at things dispassionately. It was all in disarray, stockings on the floor. It was her life. It was my life, too. It could have been my closet except for the gender of the clothes. The rusty coat hangers, the mismatched shoes, a space organized just enough to allow one to leave it for *another* space, to go out on the town, perhaps with dirty underwear.

Despite the shoddiness of our lives, did we nevertheless love each other? I suppose we did. I suppose that goes without saying. Though, in my experience, whatever goes long enough without saying, goes without existing as well.

For the first time the next night, and for the space of several minutes, we discussed the possibility of having a child. We did it the night after, too, and the next, for a total of three nights running, each time talking a little longer. The thing in the closet did not return to disturb us, though we kept the door to that closet shut. That was it. Three nights running, then no more—talk about the child, that is. Not once after that did we speak of it. That was it. Or I thought it was.

Four weeks later, we were in a shopping mall together. It was just after Christmas, the strangest time of the year. Nearly everything in the mall was on sale. We were passing a toy store.

Wait, she said.

I was somewhat confused but followed her inside. From a stack on the floor, surrounded by a little picket fence, she picked up a large box with a tiny electric train inside. The box had a cellophane top, so the train was displayed. (H.O. scale, I think it is, or was, called.) A highly detailed, little locomotive, an utterly charming thing with its little brass track. On sale, it was, but still very expensive. She took out her credit card.

In case it's a boy, she said.

We had said nothing in weeks. There had been no proposal, no further conversation, nothing whatsoever. I thought the episode had been forgotten. Her gesture came as a complete shock and surprise to me.

I said nothing. I left her standing there. I began walking up and down the devastated-looking aisles. Finally, I found what was probably the largest doll still remaining in the store. I brought it out and put it down on the counter beside the train.

In case it's a girl.

As I said, it was just after Christmas, the strangest time of the year. We became like children shopping for toys, finding the forgotten and abandoned, the unwanted things, the things on sale. Other toys, we bought, a fair number of them, also fifteen strings of Christmas lights. Not white. Not colored. But pink. The bulbs were all pink. The type of lights with the tiny clear bulbs. At such sales, one takes what remains, obviously. But it was entirely appropriate as well. After all, we were taking what remained of our lives. Like children we became.

Odd, in retrospect, but I think that what we most felt was that we were not quite *old* enough to be doing this, all alone, and without asking anyone's permission. In point of fact, we were almost *too* old, though nevertheless well within the range of parenthood.

Still, we held off actually trying.

We wanted an October child.

Other things, though, we did. We put up the Christmas lights. But not on a tree. We ran them from room to room all over her house. The bulbs were pink, as I've said; a good color, one would think, maybe even an appropriate color, to string into the teeth of fate. Along with what else? Hope? Free will? We ran the green wires from room to room, near the ceiling, on tiny brass hooks, all over her house. I still remember the rosy glow of her skin.

It never happened, though. Some of those lights may be in that very string you see behind you, for the little stage area for the bands. The lights are not all pink anymore. Most of those have burned out. That string has not been *restored* like some of the other things we have been discussing. There, you see—or I see anyway—a few at the far end of the stage. For the bands, I say—though it has been a while since any *band* has played here.

My relation to her now? It is very simple indeed. I am a customer. I sit here all night. I drink margaritas. *Salt* in the wounds, you might say.

The child never happened. Why not? Maybe life simply did not want us to escape our mess that way. But there were more proximal reasons, too; two of them, in fact, both related.

First, there were demons in her closet. At times anyway. She knew more about that than she was telling. The glint in her eyes is not necessarily from a new flame. I saw one of them, once, myself. It was near noon; I had forgotten all about the previous whisperings. I was alone in her house; I heard a slight panting noise in her bedroom, which I subconsciously dismissed as the dog—though, had I thought about it, I would have realized the *dog* was in the kitchen. I opened the door to her bedroom closet to retrieve a pair of sneakers. Then I saw it, looking suddenly dazed in the light of day. It was encrusted with sand, gargoyle-like, the size of a small baboon, with a little black leathery-looking penis, bigger than a monkey's, smaller than a man's. (They had *models*, I do believe, those medieval stone-masons). It was holding its penis in one hand. It seemed to be masturbating. There was one word to describe its affect when it saw me, looked up at me, one word only, a simple word: annoyed.

Suddenly it was gone like a rat through the hole in the floor. It was the size of a very small baboon. The face was a human face, but only in the way a *baboon*'s is a human face, or the face of your dog can be human at times. The last I saw of it was the disappearing scrape of its long pointed tail.

I must confess that what I most felt at that moment—after the first profound shock—was an enormous sense of relief—relief that I towered *over* it so. Never in this world, from the way I felt on that moonlit night would I have expected to tower *over* it.

Maybe I was overwrought (people say I was) or later *became* overwrought and thought up a reason. Many very official people have tried to convince me I did not see anything at all. It's elaborate the way they have explained it to me. I won't argue. Still, I really *did* see it, every bit as clearly as I am seeing you; moreover, this demon had an entirely different character than I could have easily made up or imagined. There was no sense whatsoever of dark depth of purpose; it seemed distracted and impromptu; it had the character, the demeanor, if you like, of an *accident*. My immediate question was how could such creatures possibly affect *real* lives. To be afraid of such a thing seemed as ludicrous to me as to be afraid of a drunk on an empty sidewalk—a drunk making his careful, staggering way home at sunrise.

What I perhaps did *not* see so clearly was the potential nature of its power; it was a power something like that of a snake, actually, probably the single most *under*appreciated power of a snake. It can get into places you cannot.

I soon found that out. Or I think I did.

Late one night, not long after, this woman and I were sound asleep when she erupted out of her dreams, screaming. I was suddenly awake as well, but disoriented, completely rattled. I was more than half-ready to start screaming myself. I had learned long ago never to touch her when she was disoriented. She does not recognize people at such times and her strength is superhuman. That night, though, I forgot; I forgot entirely; I touched her. Actually, I more than touched her. I grabbed her right hand firmly, shaking it near the head of the bed. I was frantic to wake her up. I suppose it was at that moment that she grabbed for the knife. I suppose, too, I was not nearly as silent as those limes are when it went through me (though I do believe it took three, four, five cuts, to fully register what was happening).

Indeed, I think I saw the blood before I felt the pain.

The rest of that evening is not worth imagining. What *may* be worth imagining came later; it was the intensity and power of the call to suicide which came to both of us exactly six months later and on exactly the same night.

* * *

The very last words that she actually spoke to me? Oh, that was long afterward.

But funny you should ask.

The truth is, she repeated them twice. It was many years ago. She was standing directly behind this end of the bar. I was sitting on the very stool where you see me now, having a conversation with a person on *your* stool. Actually, I do believe I was telling him the exact story I have just related. What she said, her last words to me, were these, with tears in her eyes, too:

Who are you talking to?

Who are you *talking* to?!

You act surprised. Maybe it's that I go on about her so much. I once had a urologist, a friend, as well as a bit of a philosopher, who says I was actually a victim of a dark munificence. For most men, he said, the worst scars left by a woman are internal. I am fine, now, you understand. Perfectly fine. But...my God! Look! Look at what's happening! She's coming our way! What can this possibly be about? It's probably about *you*, my friend, but we'll see! We'll see! Don't worry, I am absolutely beyond all jealousy. If it *is* about you, ignore me. Or better yet, I'll quickly get up and move. I've been very glad of the company. We've both been glad, no doubt. Without it, she and I might simply have faded away.

It's been years since anyone has come through that door to join us.

MORIYA

He's very mechanically minded.

Oh?

Yes. It's scary at times.

How so?

There is a darkness to mechanical objects that he is a bit too quick to appreciate and understand.

(The elderly lady turned ahead of them down a long hall and the mother and the boy followed. The three of them turned again, passing a shelf covered with whiskey bottles and a mahogany cabinet which the boy noticed was full of wine and single-malt scotch.)

In that case (the elderly lady said) I have something—something mechanical—that he might like to see. The girl next door wanted to see it this morning, so it's already wound.

The boy to whom the two grown women are impolite enough to be indirectly referring is fourteen years old and is following them through a Victorian-looking house on his first day in New Orleans. He is to take six weeks of intensive French lessons in a special summer program for adolescents in a school on Jackson Avenue. The elderly woman is a moderately-distant friend of his mother's who is going to put him up and who is leading both of them now into a parlor tinkling with prisms and light.

Indeed, the idea of "something mechanical" immediately had this boy's interest. Just as immediately, he saw it and was disappointed. Enough so, that it was difficult to fully conceal his disappointment. The mechanical thing was a clock. It was a glass clock in the center of a marble table. It was ticking steadily. The clock had an exposed mechanism, a pendulum weighted with dual glass tubes full of mercury, but otherwise was of a rather familiar style and unremarkable. There were some other antiquated objects in the room, some family pictures in ornate somewhat brassy-looking shadow-box frames, a spinet-style piano, two medallion sofas facing one another beneath a third medallion on the ceiling. Indeed, there was something of a medallion "theme" to the entire center of the parlor. It is unlikely that the boy would have known or noticed this. He was, after all, mechanically, not architecturally minded. On the left-hand sofa, however, there was something he *did* notice, couldn't help but, a doll, a virtually life-sized doll, not a "baby" doll either but a doll representing an adolescent girl, a girl in her mid-adolescence, perhaps. Had she been standing up she might have been over four feet high, perhaps well over. She was wearing a nineteenth-century, European, many-buttoned, fin-de-siècle dress, a maroon velvet jacket and some high-topped black shoes. She had been positioned so that she was looking somewhat wistfully out of a long French window, one elbow on the arm of the sofa. There was a black ribbon with a medallion on it around her neck.

(The boy went dutifully to the clock.)

We think a Swiss clock-maker made it, the woman continued. It's from 1892, over a hundred years old at this point.

The boy looked at the beveled glass, the spattering of color on the marble table-top, the mercury-filled tubes, and stood there waiting for the woman to say something more about it. Actually, though, he knew the theory of the tubes himself. Heat causes metal to expand and the pendulum being metal will lengthen, lowering the center of gravity and therefore slowing the clock—not much, of course, infinitesimally, as a matter of fact, but when one is counting seconds over months or years the differences become significant, then profound. The mercury in the tubes is confined so that it can only expand upward, *raising* the center of gravity so the effects cancel.

(Well, he thought, standing patiently, politely, at the table, at least he could show off his knowledge.)

Is this the original key? he said.

What?

It was only then that the boy realized that the woman was neither looking at him nor the clock.

Oh, that, she said. Not *that*. I know nothing about that. That's new, for *us* anyway. That was at an estate sale last year. Sit down.

Ma'am?

Sit down. Here. The woman patted the sofa beside her, rubbed the red velvet flirtatiously, made room between herself and the boy's mother.

This woman, with her well-applied makeup and at least one face-lift, was elegant in the slightly decadent manner of the best-preserved of sixty-year-old females. She was the sort of woman who can successfully squeeze the last remnants of sensuality out of age, possessing, still, the power of crossed legs in cocktail dresses, knowing well the uses of black chiffon, gold jewelry, French perfume and alcohol. In fact, bringing a fourteen-year-old into a parlor tinkling with such temptations might have given many a mother pause. But this particular woman had a husband she was still moderately crazy about, a handsome lawyer with an alcoholic nose who was a member of one of the old-line Mardi Gras krewes and a fixture at Galatoire's on Friday. (In fact, the husband was there now, this being a Friday.) So that particular story is possibly over before it starts.

Wait, the woman said, facing the other sofa now.

The doll continued looking out the window. The clock continued ticking on its table.

The boy sat down, began waiting, leaned forward slightly.

It may take a while. Would you like a Coca-Cola?

The boy was equally puzzled by both sentences.

He was still facing the sofa. He had already noticed that the two sofas were not quite identical. The one the doll was on was slightly longer and had darker, somewhat different-looking woodwork. He was beginning to make other comparisons. But, at that moment, the doll began to turn. She began to turn toward him, slowly, as he watched, though not so slowly as to be unlifelike. It was as though she had been interrupted in the midst of a daydream. Her brilliant hazel eyes were not fixed, not what they call "doll-like," they moved independently of her head and slightly in advance of it, giving an effect the realism of which was uncanny. Her hazel-colored eyes were crystalline, maybe literally. There was no movement of her mouth, which, like her face, was ceramic, or ivory, or alabaster and *was* doll-like, though the lips were full and there was a feeling and even a glimpse of natural teeth. She moved her elbow and left hand from the armrest and crossed both hands (politely?) in her lap. She was wearing long white gloves which, had her jacket been removed, would have proved to extend past her elbows. She moved her right hand and tugged on the fabric of her left glove as though to straighten it or exorcise some ghost of disorder.

Then she looked at the boy again, directly at him, through him. There could have been no more steadfast stare. The most saucy and impudent thirteen-year-old that has ever taken the perilous step of trying the effects of lipstick on a stepfather could not have had such a gaze. The doll had a breathtaking face, not innocent, but breathtaking: high cheekbones, shadowy eyes, dark hair that seemed real. His own gaze flinched down somewhat to the black-and-white medallion around her neck. Her breasts were so well-formed, her blouse so tucked-in as to give a sense of suspended breathing.

The woman was talking to his mother now.

It's the only one like it we've ever seen. It's Swiss, we think. It stayed in the attic for decades in a cedar-lined box. It was in my husband Eric's family. Eric's grandfather would have had to know something about it, since this was his house and furniture. Eric himself says he had never seen it before. His grandfather never mentioned the thing, had forgotten about it, perhaps, or perhaps kept it a secret deliberately, since he had three daughters in addition to his son. Maybe he wanted to avoid a fight. We didn't find it till a few months ago. The year 1892 was stamped on—actually burned into—the wood of the box. It was in an alcove under an unbelievable number of blankets.

(The women, of course, are talking around the boy again.)

The crank is in that case, the woman said, pointing to a narrow leather box. There are a number of movements it goes through randomly, *sometimes* randomly, sometimes not. I'm not sure that we've seen them all as yet. It seems, at times, that where you touch it very much affects the internal program. You may touch it, if you like.

The boy came closer but could hear no sound of clockwork. The doll's eyes had not moved, her head had not moved, still she seemed to be following him. He grasped the tips of her gloved fingers, tremulously, as though shaking hands, as though saying hello.

After a moment, the doll turned slightly and looked up at him. Her eyes, once again, slightly leading the movement. It was impossible to believe it was coincidental.

It will run for days, the woman said. The spring must be enormous. It *feels* enormous when you wind it.

What's her name?

My God! You're the second person who has asked that today! Actually, we haven't named her. Or maybe we have.

My husband and I have begun calling her "the doll." You can name her if you like.

(The boy was still waiting, still holding the doll's hand.)

Can you stop her? he said. Her motion, I mean. Is it possible to shut her off?

(Outside the house, he heard the shriek of a young girl's voice next door.)

Yes, there's a little wheel in the back of her neck, just under the ribbon.

The boy went behind her, behind the sofa and rested both his hands on the doll's shoulders. Her eyelashes were almost assuredly real, her hair, too, human, straight, long and luxurious. It seemed he could smell a trace of perfume. He looked down at the fabric of her dress, felt the little wheel beneath the ribbon.

Interesting, the woman said. See what I mean? (The woman was talking to the boy's mother now.) I've never seen her do that before.

The doll was turning around to look at the boy. She succeeded, too, to a surprising degree, finishing by staring up at him, her neck arched slightly.

During the first week, the boy attempted to make a complete catalog of the doll's movements. She seldom moved as much as she had the first day. Sometimes, she would go a full hour or two without any motion of any kind. He would come into the parlor in the afternoon or evening and watch her and wait. Her activity was completely unpredictable: five minutes, thirty minutes, forty-seven and a half minutes between movements. Then she might do a lot, an entire series of things, as though bored by the long inactivity—straighten a glove, adjust her knees, slap at an invisible fly. The most elaborate thing she could do was the following: put both hands down, curl her knuckles slightly, and lift her entire body a fraction of an inch to the right. But before that motion was ever repeated, she would move to the left again, so that there was no overall change in position. Often, she would fold her hands together, waiting; and from that position move her eyes, alone, so as to look slowly around the room. (Literally, she seemed very much to *look* at something for a while, then at something else.) Occasionally, she would look down at the floor for quite a period of time, so that one would be very tempted to say: "This little doll once had a little dog."

Her eyes themselves, the boy noticed, seemed as though they should be able to close, the lids seemed to be hinged, or *potentially* hinged, but they never did, or he never saw them do it. They never blinked, even. He could hear her ticking only by holding his ear directly on her body, but anyplace on it, would work, her back, for instance, or one of her shoulders. There was quite a *presence* in the sound, not a slow tick.....tick.....tick....tick...like a clock; but something faster, shorter, more breathless and passionate: a tic-tic-tic-tic-tic-tic-tic-tic-tic, full in its own way, of the quality of construction, of the click of micrometers, of the precise cut of lathes, of the tempering of steel for shafts and mainsprings.

The boy had other concerns, of course. Before leaving home, he had had daydreams that there might be some girl in New Orleans waiting just for him. But those dreams did not pan out. All the girls were older. He was literally the youngest individual in his class. Most of the girls had boyfriends with driver's licenses. They were friendly enough but definitely not interested in any fourteen-year-old "mechanically-minded" boy. On several occasions, he hunted for but did not find the girl next door, nor, for that matter, did he ever hear her again.

Under the circumstances, the question that became paramount for him was how long the doll would run. It dawned on him that it might be somewhat difficult to tell. The doll might continue to *tick* long after she had stopped moving because it should take less energy to do that. In fact, every day, after class, he would wonder, has she stopped already?

He began to leave things in her hands, little bits of paper, to see if she had moved in his absence. Infinitesimal, these pieces of paper were, some of them virtually the size of lint. He would find them later, on the sofa, on the armrest, on the floor beneath her feet. After a while, he began writing tiny messages on them. To camouflage, as far as possible, what he was doing he would write very small, so that what she ended up holding was an unreadable blob of ink. But in each case *he* knew what he had written and was pleased to think she did as well.

Hello.

Thinking of you.

Sleep well.

Or:

I think you're beautiful.

Will try to dream of Switzerland for your sake.

(He would find the messages on the cushion of the sofa, on the armrest, on the floor beneath her feet.)

The boy *did* try to dream of Switzerland for her; and, in order to get a focus for his dream, saturated himself with ideas and images of the area from two sets of encyclopedias in the house: pictures of the Alps, of cows, of cheese, of Zurich and Bern. He thought that perhaps she might come *alive* for him in a dream.

(And, as he began to learn more French, he tried speaking to her.)

Je t'aime.

On the sofa sometimes, unmoving for hours, he would stare at her, trying to saturate his brain with her beauty. Her hazel eyes were so realistic it was impossible to believe she was not seeing him too, watching him, waiting for something.

Nothing came of the dreams, though. That is, they did not happen.

In truth, the two of them didn't get much time absolutely alone together. Other things would intervene. The maid would come in. The husband would enter with his pipe, the wife with her cigarettes, or both, simultaneously. They seemed, mainly, to smoke in that room. The boy noticed one evening that the doll was looking directly at the husband as he fiddled with his pipe and he suddenly realized he was feeling something very like jealousy.

One afternoon, while waiting for the doll to move, he began looking at the family pictures in the shadow-box frames. He noticed there was a resemblance, a definite resemblance, between this doll and certain of the women in the pictures. He thought they might be the wives. The maid came on Tuesdays and Thursdays and he began to ask her questions. She knew the answers to most of them and the woman eventually provided him with the rest. He found that the daughters in the family had *some*thing of a resemblance, passed on, no doubt, genetically; but what he had guessed initially was the truth. The real resemblance was to the wives.

The boy opened the leather box, looked at the crank with its mahogany handle, lifted it up, set it back. There were some spare buttons for the blouse, a long Allen wrench with a T-shaped handle, some regular wrenches, too, three screwdrivers, a button hook. (There was also an impression of these things crushed into the velvet lining of the top of the box.)

How long could the spring *last?* he wondered. It was already more than "days" as the woman had suggested. It was "weeks," now, past two, and well into a third. But then it quit. The boy came home one afternoon and found his last message (unread?) in her hand. The doll had run down. She was stopped, frozen, dead, caught in the middle of a motion. It was a most unnatural-looking position for her, her eyes on the floor, her neck in the process of a turn. Seeing it, he immediately understood the importance of a little-appreciated role and function of funeral directors, who have as their responsibility the final, strictly physical, disposition of a human body: the adjusting of hands and feet, the closing of eyes, the stopping of life at a node.

The boy felt strongly that the doll shouldn't be left like this. Did they even notice, the man and woman? Why *didn't* they? Maybe they weren't really looking at her. He decided he would rewind her himself. He decided he would fix the problem.

It would be three days before he could do that, though. The man and woman were going to dinner at Commander's Palace on Saturday. Afterward, they were going to a party in the French Quarter. He would have two full hours at least, maybe more, maybe considerably more.

(In the meantime, she sat there, gathering infinitesimal dust.)

Saturday evening he waited a full twenty minutes after they left. Then he waited another ten in case they had forgotten something. Finally, he went into the parlor, locked the doors, closed the curtains and opened the box of tools. He saw the mahogany handle, the black velvet lining, noted, in passing almost, that the top section of the box (where the images of the tools were crushed) was somewhat thicker than it had to be. He realized the velvet lining of the case might hold or conceal something, might, in fact, fold down (*did* fold down he discovered with the aid of a bent paper clip). What he saw immediately inside was a certificate.

The certificate had a name, *Moriya*, printed in ornate black script at the top. There was some more writing, too, near that, in a smaller, different script: Austral Kraftwerk, Prague. Then there was a paragraph of print and some hand-written specifications in an antique and purple-looking ink in a series of printed blanks. The writing might have been German, might have been Czech. He did not know. He had had two years of Latin and now, of course, a smattering of French. But he had no idea. Austral Kraftwerk, Prague. What he saw now was that the design on the medallion on the doll's neck was the trademark for the company. Not one word of the writing was meaningful to him. There was a serial number and part of a decorative scroll around the edge of the certificate. One of the bottom corners of the scroll had been torn off. He thought there might once have been an engraved picture of the doll in that corner. If so, it had been torn off. Why had it been torn off?

The boy thought that there might have been such a picture because there was something *else* engraved on the other corner, something totally unexpected: the sofa! But of course! The sofa was part of the doll! Not connected, obviously, but a platform for it, as it obviously had to be. Probably the doll had to be placed at the end of it, at the far left end, too. There might be things inside it, magnets, for instance, that allowed the doll to orient herself. Who, then, in this family had known to put her there? Someone was not telling the whole truth here.

Well, well, well, he thought. So, then, the doll's name was Moriya.

"Moriya," he said, coming around in front and looking at her, touching her fingertips.

But she continued to look dead to him, distorted; and, of course, there was no movement of her eyes.

Still, the boy realized, it was very possible that only *he* knew the rest of the story. This doll had not been made in Switzerland; she had been made in Prague. His hands were slightly tremulous now as he began to undress her. He was worried, at first, about how to handle her arms; but her maroon velvet jacket unhooked in the back, came off immediately, he discovered. He unlaced the back of the dress, which also came apart easily. The dress had innumerable pleats and revealed underneath what he would have called a black corset; but which the woman, outside of the house now, would have known was a bustier. The boy saw that he didn't have to remove that. There was a hole in the fabric itself in the low back. As a precaution, though, before he inserted the crank, he moved the wheel in her neck to the "off" position. He inserted the short, stubby, but rather massive crank and began to turn it. He was expecting a heavy sound like click...click...click. What he heard, instead, had more of a roaring quality and feel. He wound it on and on, tighter and tighter: ten, twelve, fifteen, twenty, thirty, a total of forty times before the spring began to feel really tight to him. At the end, he relaxed the crank very carefully to be sure the ratchet would hold. Then he turned the wheel in her neck and watched as she completed the turn she had begun days ago. She came to rest in a position he had seen many times before, her eyes slightly averted. Was she being shy? Flirtatious?

Disheveled now, her jacket down, her young back showing, what he saw was the breathtaking, incredible modeling of her scapulas and vertebrae. Her skin was not ceramic, but what was it? Ivory? Alabaster? It was something that looked like ivory to him. It was slightly warm-feeling. He saw the dark bustier, the stunning shoulder blades, the pleated cloth hanging off her right shoulder, and all of a sudden the temptation became too great for him.

He began to undo the front of her dress.

The little fabric-covered buttons were somewhat difficult to manipulate. He saw it would be rather easy to break one. The doll's breasts were not overly large. Her nipples were of a deeper hue than her lips. Her pigments were getting darker, it seemed, in the more caudal direction (a word he would not have known but a principle he might have appreciated). What he noticed about the breasts was that they were not unfinished. The doll's breasts, like her back, were perfect; they were not just forms and armatures for fabric; they were meant to be seen. He began to see very clearly now; this doll was not designed around a dress. She was designed around a nude body.

The doll's nipples were of a rubbery material, darkly pink. Where the rubber came together centrally, it could be pulled and teased apart. It dawned on him that something might be hidden beneath the rubber. Screws perhaps. This might be the way to take off the front of the doll.

The boy was well familiar with the deviousness of mechanical constructions. In disassembling such things as vacuum cleaners, radios, televisions and lawn mowers, he had learned long ago (virtually in kindergarten, in fact) that the innocent-looking moldings and chrome strips frequently hid the mounting attachments for a motor or chassis. This was wildly different, of course; yet, all things considered, it was right up his alley. He turned the doll off, ran to the kitchen, and got a flashlight. With the light, he looked carefully as he pried gently into the rubber nipples with the tip of the buttonhook. No, there were no screw heads. The holes went deeper, though, so maybe something else would fit. The Allen wrench, perhaps. It was possible that he was on the right track. Another thought, though, was beginning to bother him. Would a dress of this era normally lace in the back and *button* in front? He had no idea.

It seemed this doll's clothes were made to be taken off quickly.

Behind him, on the marble table, the clock continued to tick. The boy was taking rather more time with all of this than he realized. And now, in his rush to get the flashlight, he had left the door to the parlor unlocked.

He took the T-shaped Allen wrench out of the case and tried to insert it directly through the rubber in the right nipple. He was not successful. He met resistance immediately. Still, to be thorough, he tried it in the left as well. It went in. Not a little. It went in the full length of the shaft.

With one hand on her back and one hand on the T-shaped handle, he now had a decision to make: whether or not to turn the wrench. The doll's eyes were still averted. This could possibly cause her body to spring open. He might not be able to get her back together again. There was no clue as to what was going to happen. He waited several seconds thinking, deliberating, resting his full palm flat against her bare back. Then the doll's eyes began to move. They moved upward a matter of millimeters and began to drift steadily to the right toward him. It was a move he had never seen her make before. Finally, her eyes met his, not exactly but almost. He leaned down to intersect her gaze. It was impossible to believe she was not seeing him, talking to him, begging him silently. He took a quick breath and turned the handle clockwise. Nothing happened. Absolutely nothing. He met complete resistance. (Actually, he was almost relieved to find it.) Then (being very thorough again) he turned the handle the other way.

Something clunked deep within the interior of the doll. Deep within the doll, he heard something rather heavy-sounding move into another position.

The boy listened quickly, almost desperately, holding his ear to her bare shoulder. There was no change whatsoever in the noise (tic-tic-tic-tic-tic-tic-tic-tic-tic). Then again, maybe there *was*. Maybe the ticking was faster now.

The boy held the Allen wrench in his hand, waiting, but nothing happened. He sat down beside her, still nothing. He looked at the clock on the table. Fifteen minutes, he thought.

He waited beside her, the doll with her breasts bared, her black bustier open. She seemed to be looking toward but not directly at the clock. A woman ignoring you might look in such a direction. Suddenly, the boy remembered the unlocked door. He jumped up, ran to lock it, sat down again.

He should be safe, anyway, he thought, should have plenty of time. They should still be at Commander's Palace now. He should have plenty...hours, maybe. On the other hand, what if they dropped by *here* on the way to the Quarter.

Fifteen minutes, he thought.

But it didn't take that long.

After six minutes of ticking, the doll blinked. Actually, what the doll did was a good deal more than a blink; it was slower, and more prolonged:

She fully closed and opened her eyes.

Then she began to move her right hand. The doll moved her right hand forward and set it down rather firmly near the boy's knee and began to pull along his leg and thigh. She did not stop. She pulled steadily and directly into his crotch and stayed there for a long time. What she was doing now was evidently not unintentional. She was steadily moving her hand. The boy did not know whether to look at her or not. He could barely see her dark and tender lashes. Then he felt her hand on his shoulder. The doll had changed positions somewhat; she had put her gloved hand on his left shoulder and leaned into him. This was an entirely different, beseeching, sort of movement. In a human being you would say that what was wanted now was a kiss; the girl—or lady—wants a kiss. In a doll, of course, you could not say that, not accurately that is. But the boy said it anyway. He kissed her. He kissed her on her mouth. The doll's mouth was not unpleasant feeling. Her mouth was electrifying. She looked up, seemed to lock onto his eyes. He felt more and more pressure in her kiss, more and more and more of the pressure. Then he realized what what happening.

The doll was climbing on top of him. The boy fell the full length of the sofa and her sudden, unexpected heaviness was upon him. Her dark hair fell completely over both of them. By helping her slightly he got her legs on the sofa, too, and centered in his groin area. She was as heavy as a small sack of fertilizer. Altogether, the sensation was unexpected, weird and magical; she *felt* real. Not that he had ever felt a girl in this situation. But then again there was no object that had ever felt like *this*. Her balance was perfect. He had already been phenomenally, wildly, turned on by the kiss alone. With this extra activity, he was reaching unprecedented heights (or lengths). But he didn't feel any receptacle for what had now grown between them. Steadily, powerfully the doll began to grind against him. Her searching eyes locked firmly onto his. He felt desperately, but her groin was perfectly smooth. He inserted his hand down beneath her clothes to make absolutely sure. There was nothing. She continued to pin him with her mouth and grind against him. What must such a doll have *cost?* was almost his last thought before he exploded into his own underwear. She ground into him for another full minute, then stopped, leaving him with her weight and the warm, soapy stickiness.

Je t'aime, the boy said. J'ai la tête de la mécanique.

The doll's eyes remained closed, as though sleeping. The boy put his hand on the back of her head. He stayed on the sofa an additional ten minutes, feeling her satisfying weight, the slight vibration of her body, all fear of being discovered gone, the glass clock on the table steadily ticking, all centers of gravity in the room perfectly balanced now. The boy waited another five minutes, even afterward, vaguely curious, vaguely thinking something else might happen. But nothing did.

At last the boy sat up, then sat *her* up and turned her off. Her dress was still more or less in place. But he wanted to take a closer look at her groin area. There was nothing there, nothing. The area was perfectly smooth, sexless in a way, an ivory groin. No, wait a minute. There was *some*thing but it was not a part of her. There was something *written*, embroidered in the cloth of her underpants (they didn't really look like panties to him but it was the last garment before her bare body). The writing was in script in dark letters, a phrase in Latin:

Talis umbras mundum regnant.

The boy smiled and said it aloud, musingly. So, the sole use, thus far, in his life, of two full years of Latin was to understand the message written on a doll's underpants. He began to put the doll back together. He checked carefully for stains. All was fine, perfect; no stains, nothing. Finally, with the Allen wrench, he set her back to the clockwise position, waited a moment, looking.

The doll suddenly opened her eyes.

He kissed her and turned off the light.

Have you thought of a name for her?

No.

(This was three days later, in the parlor, where the boy was sitting after class, studying a list of verbs. The woman had come in to retrieve a pack of cigarettes from a carton.)

The boy was shocked at how quickly he had been able to lie, to think of all the unknowns and ramifications and know the name he now had for her, *her* name in fact, could never be said. It was one of those moments in life that he knew, for sure, that he was developing the adult mind.

I think "the doll" is a perfectly fine name, he said, watching the woman.

The woman fished a pack of cigarettes from a carton. (Even *she* resembled the doll; could she possibly not *see* that?)

Who thought of putting her on the sofa? the boy said.

Oh? You think she looks good there?

Yes.

My husband.

Four times, and four times only, the boy and Moriya were able to intersect. During the last two, the boy was bare from the waist down and Moriya was almost perfectly nude. By diligently searching up and down Magazine Street, he had found a filling station with a condom machine in the restroom. He had bought several; they were a bit large, of course; still, they simplified certain worries—not so *much* of a problem, after all, for a fourteen-year-old, but enough for staining a sofa or a dress.

All through the days that followed, the boy had more energy than he had ever had in his life. He felt more *alive*.

He would watch Moriya in the afternoon light, the saucy, impudent, perfectly beautiful face, the risqué and hungry mouth, cherish the memory and anticipation of her ivory groin grinding into his. In the actual sexual encounters, it helped to know, now, exactly what was going to happen, when her hand was going to move, when she was going to need assistance with her feet.

Since the boy now knew where Moriya was *really* from, he decided to try the trick of the dream again. It worked, too, this time, and magnificently. (But once, and once only.) He sneaked a heavy volume of the encyclopedia to bed with him and read the entire article about Prague, twice through, completely, just before turning out the light. Sure enough, during the night she came to him. Or, more correctly, *he* went to her. He went to Prague. He and Moriya were suddenly walking across the Charles Bridge together. She was tracing the veins in his hand with her gloved hand.

Then they were in a cafe, each with a glass of wine.

I have a *secret*, she said.

(There was a light heaviness to her voice; it was precisely articulate, as though English were her third or fourth language.)

What? he said.

She was bubbling over with excitement.

But she would not tell him.

I know a *secret!* she said again, later. She came around the little table and sat on his lap, dangling her feet above the ceramic tiles. She pressed the tips of her fingers into his cheeks, head-to-head, nose-to-nose, her eyes locked onto his, to fix and center his vision. There was an incredible glow of energy around her. She leaned forward as though to whisper something, but licked his ear instead.

Interestingly, the boy's dream was not set in 1892, not in the era of gaslights and horses, the era of her construction, but in a strange and intermediate time. It would have had to have been somewhere in the 1930s just before the second world war. There were only a few cars, very dark, dusty. But what cars! What magnificent machines! He saw a fair number of Mercedes, a couple of Rolls Royces (the great roadsters and dual-cowled phaetons), a Bugatti, an Invicta, an Hispano-Suiza. The cars were parked on the stone bridges, the stone streets, the horses clopping by them. The greatest cars of the twentieth century, covered with dust from the road.

It was a mechanically minded dream.

But four times, and four times only, the two of them had together. Not that that was absolutely all the possible chances. It was because on the last chance something disastrous happened.

The man and woman were going to another party (in Covington, this time, across Lake Pontchartrain and The Causeway).

The boy knew he would have plenty of time.

Thirty minutes after they'd left, he had the doll perfectly nude. But with such a luxury of time, he began to look at her more carefully. On her flanks now, he saw several other places for the Allen wrench to insert, a total of six of them, between her arms and her waist. This had to be the way to get inside her. The boy's curiosity began to get the better of him. There was so much she could *do* and he couldn't begin to imagine how. He simply had to *see*, first-hand, what was going on. He quickly removed six long machine screws with hexagonal insert heads and set them on the marble-topped table. He managed to get his fingernails into a seam in her back and then, with the smallest screwdriver, pry her alabaster skin up carefully, very carefully so as not to crack it. He had to break a sort of suction. He could scarcely pull the skin off. This doll had probably not been opened in a hundred years. He saw some green felt, some brass gears, some shafting; then, suddenly, an incredible surprise: Wires! Electrical wires! Yellow, cotton-covered wires! Bundles of them, everywhere, even attached to her back through a very odd-looking detachable connector. There was a flywheel between the doll's shoulder blades. It was not spinning, though, and would *not* spin even when he released the control in her neck. He suspected some chunks of unmachined metal that he saw near the flywheel might be magnets, and tested one of them with the blade of the screwdriver:

It was all he could do to pull it away again.

A magnet indeed, a very powerful magnet! What he was looking at was a dynamo. This doll generated her own electricity! There were several copper discs attached to the underside of her skin. He saw a number of others inside, too, maybe an eighth of an inch thick, maybe thicker, and a couple of inches in diameter. For what? Capacitance effects? Probably not, at least not in this era. On the other hand, thermocouples were a definite possibility. Thermocouples were really old, he knew; he had seen a book from the 1880s that had them in it. Thermocouples would be sensitive to heat, too, or to *changes* in heat. So she *could* know when and where she was being touched.

There was absolutely no dust, though. The doll's body might have been sealed yesterday. Only the dullness of the brass and some corrosion of the bearings revealed her true age. So moisture itself can enter, the boy thought (or perhaps it simply condensed inside her). He saw shafts with differential gearing and hard-rubber wheels pressing against discs to give integrals and derivatives of motion. Along her flanks, and in the back side of her breasts, there were areas where lead had been cast to give the proper weight distribution. All of this was so much more elaborate than he could have dreamed. There were banks of wire-wound resistors in what appeared to be a series of Wheatstone bridges, arranged, perhaps, in a sort of decision tree. (Wouldn't you need to *amplify* the current though? Maybe not.) What must such a doll have *cost*? he thought. Her movements themselves were powered by the spring; but many of the decisions were evidently electromechanical. Not all of them, though, because he saw a cylindrical stack of metal discs with slots, like in a music box, tiny relays, strain gauges, electromagnetic clutches. The doll had to be pushing the absolute *limits* of the technology of the era. Still, the great majority of the time everything was evidently disengaged; she sat there ticking steadily, declutched and waiting.

(Tic-tic-tic-tic-tic-tic-tic-tic-tic.)

The boy sat the doll up and put her, very carefully now, in the counter-clockwise position, since the motions were continuous there and he knew what they would be. The flywheel of the dynamo suddenly began to spin. He could slow it, stop it, though, by touching the escapement wheel. The escapement was finer-toothed than a clock's. Every time he put his finger down on the wheel, the doll's hand would stop. If he let it go, it would run. It would run, then stop, run then stop. Tic-tic-tic-tic....tic-tic... He was watching the part of the movement where she would normally grab for his shoulder. But this time there was going to be no shoulder for her to grab. With his finger he had complete control of her: Tic-tic-tic....tic-tic....tic-tic. She moved now an inch, now a quarter of an inch, now a matter of millimeters. Something seemed to have been filtered out of the movement, though. Something very real but difficult to describe. What? Well. *Some*thing. Passion maybe. It seemed to be passion.

Was passion some function of time?

She would run, then stop, run then stop: tic-tic-tic-tic.... tic-tic. Her movements had become somewhat jerky at this speed. The boy was utterly fascinated. He found himself watching the tremor of her gloved hand. Had he inadvertently *aged* the doll? He touched her again and again, letting her move only incrementally. Tic....tic.....tic...... tic...................tic

At that moment, the escapement wheel sheared off. It sheared completely off and dropped deep within the mechanism. What was left of the little shaft began to spin furiously. The gloved hand of the doll shot eight inches in less than a second. The boy's sense of panic could not have been greater had there been an artery spurting blood across the room. He quickly grabbed at the other control in her neck, stopped the motion, stopped the shaft, his heart pounding furiously.

Oh my God!

He couldn't get to the wheel. It had fallen deep inside. He could not reach it within the labyrinth of machinery. The boy tilted the doll, shook her a little, righted her. There was a tinkling springy noise as the wheel fell down and lodged somewhere near the bottom. It would take a major disassembly to get to it now and would do no good whatsoever since the shaft itself was broken.

There was absolutely no way to put the wheel back.

The boy stood there, terrified. In desperation, he tried inserting the wrench and turning her back to the clockwise position. He thought there possibly might be a second escapement for that position. (Just possibly.) At the same time, he knew in his heart, that that would never be true. Absolutely knew, even before he turned the wrench. It was impossible. And yet there *was*. He heard it as soon as he released the control. There was indeed *another* escapement ticking more deeply inside her. He waited, sat her up, her back still open, waited, waited (tic-tic-tic). Suddenly, she began to move. The normal position seemed to be OK. The boy held his ear close to her shoulder. (Tic-tic-tic-tic-tic-tic-tic.) The sound was exactly the same as always. The normal position was OK, or seemed to be. He began sealing her shut again.

After all, he thought, perhaps no one *knew* about the other position. Working furiously, he began to put Moriya back together. The precision of this doll's construction was absolutely unbelievable. He had to wait to let air escape before the two halves would seal together. He was virtually spinning the Allen wrench now, his hands moving as accurately as a surgeon's. Soon, there was no trace whatsoever of his entering, no felt showing, no misalignment. It was all snug, tight, perfect.

The boy began to dress her, then to lace up her bustier. He had a sense that his time was limited, that something *else* was about to go wrong. He laced up the back of her dress, missed one position and had to start again. The normal position was OK, he thought, and perhaps no one knew about the other. Or, if they *did*, they might assume they had broken her themselves. He straightened her dress, began to hook her velvet jacket. Get her dressed! Get her *dressed!* *Hurry!* he thought. The normal position is OK he told himself (or *was* telling himself) until a question brought him up short in his thoughts:

Exactly which position was normal?

He finished hooking up her velvet jacket and quickly turned out the light.

There had been absolutely no need to rush. It was several hours before the man and woman returned. Still, afterward, for three full days, the boy worried himself sick about the doll. Why? Because of the escapement wheel. How could he be sure it was completely out of the way? For all possible movements, that is. It might still strip a gear or cause something to short-circuit. The boy studiously avoided entering the parlor. He didn't want to be physically in the same room if something within Moriya began to grind and malfunction. Each day before class, he looked in to see whether or not she had moved. When he was home, he went past the parlor doorway, nervously, almost hourly. Had she changed position? Yes. No. Maybe. Yes. (Yes, indeed.) The doll seemed to be running perfectly. Still, he could not study for worrying. All he thought of in class now was Moriya, alone, in that parlor, initiating each perilous new motion. Three days, four days, five days, six. She

should have gone through most of her program now. The
man and woman would go into the parlor, leave it, notice
nothing, say nothing. Mostly, though, Moriya sat there all
alone. The boy would watch her from the hall. He, too,
noticed absolutely nothing. Indeed, it seemed absolutely
nothing had changed.

But in those days of worry and despair, he began to see the
doll in a new light, as something of an agent, ambassador
and spy. What kind of reasoning had gone into her? What
was she all about? Her design was more than clever; it was
demonic in its brilliance, compulsive in its perfection; perhaps
the work of some famously dirty-minded old clockmaker
from the Austral *Kraft*werk in Prague who had sent her into
the world in search of fourteen-year-old boys. From this
point of view, the boy saw that he had been set up, framed,
completely. There was nothing necessarily gentle or bright
here. What dark imperatives was this doll fulfilling? The boy
could imagine a shop with lathes and drill presses, wires and
electromagnets, petticoats and steel filings—pipes too, and
cheese, micrometers, and tankards of beer. What was *he*
thinking of (the clockmaker) when he had designed her? Was
he dreaming of the sex himself? And, if so, with whom? Was
it *his* hand that found its way up your leg? After all, the
message on the underwear was not from her but from the
clockmaker: Talis Umbras Mundum Regnant. *That* was a
message from the clockmaker, wasn't it?

The feeling did not last long. Another feeling soon replaced
it in the boy's heart. The new feeling was loneliness, a
bottomless loneliness, the most abject loneliness imaginable.
He went through a daily agony. It was as though *he* were
broken, not she. He would stand at the door, watch her adjust
her position, straighten her glove, scratch an invisible fly off a
sleeve. She was trapped now. *He* was trapped without her.
His misery and guilt became unbearable. After dinner one
evening, he realized he simply had to go in to see her again.
Cautious, shy, nervous, he tucked his shirttail in, actually

checked his appearance in a mirror, before he went through the door. He sat down on the opposite sofa with his French book as though nothing had happened. He waited there nervously. *Why* was he nervous? What was this, silliness? Superstition? She was a *toy*, wasn't she? At last the doll began to turn and look directly at him. He held his breath as her eyes met his. Then he saw her, truly saw her, for the first time in a week. Her face. He had forgotten it. He had *not* forgotten it. He had... He went numb inside.

He went.

Then she continued her turn beyond him, seemed, at last, to be looking at something out the door. She adjusted her glove, became motionless once more.

She did not move again for two hours.

She was trapped now. *He* was trapped without her. The doll did not look at him again. She seemed to avert her eyes.

The boy's dream of Prague came back to him. What secret could she have had? What could it have possibly been? That she loved him? That she was pregnant? What could it have been?

It was an agony to remember it. It was simply too painful to think about.

There was nothing now, nothing. The doll would adjust her gloves, straighten them, fold her hands, look up, look down, and just about break his heart.

I have insulted her, he thought, with these thoughts of a clockmaker. He had met *her* in Prague, or at least had met something that very much *seemed* to be her. They had talked. She had talked *to* him. *She* was not bound by those wires. There was something, a shadow of something, within her that got beyond everything, beyond the gears, the shafts, the magnets—an umbra, so to speak; *umbras* the plural would be. Was that her secret? Was that what she had wanted and not wanted to tell him? *Talis umbras mundum regnant.* ("Such shadows rule the world.") He could not have had that dream without her.

Did she say she *knew* a secret or *had* a secret?

His memory of the dream was already fading.

And then his French course was over.

And then there was the afternoon he came to visit her for the last time. He felt the briefest flush of hope when he entered the room. Everything was not perfectly gloomy. What can be broken, can be fixed, he thought. What can be broken, can be fixed. There was a dimension to all of this he had to ignore, a reality, if you will. But a balance wheel can be reattached, a shaft can be machined, from scratch if necessary. Still, it would be too late for him. The normal, or maybe *not* the normal, part of the doll still worked perfectly. The other could be fixed. But not for him, never for him, fixed or not, *that* was gone forever. He would never be in this parlor again, never have another chance, never be on the sofa with this girl, never feel her pressure against him, never see her close her eyes like a kitten to sleep.

The dangling prisms weighed heavily on his soul. The doll sat on her sofa, perfectly motionless. He stood there, watching her, breathing mainly out of his mouth. "Je t'aime," he said, quietly.

It had been impossible, over the days, not to see longing, then reproach, then anger in those eyes.

He would leave tomorrow. He told her that. (Out loud, in fact.) He waited, waited a long time. She did not move.

Je t'aime. I love you, he said again, finally.

The doll still did not move. She continued staring out the window. She did not believe him anymore.

The boy picked up some papers that he had left in the parlor and walked toward the front of the house. He heard, outside, in another world, another block, the shriek of some children. On the spur of the moment, he decided to go out onto the front porch. He saw the street lamps, the live oaks, stood there quietly, glum and melancholy. There was a solid hedge of boxwood in front of him and to his right.

The loveliness of the afternoon was almost but not completely lost on him.

Did she say I have or I *know*? he thought.

Strange, in six weeks, he had scarcely been on this porch. He stood there, patiently, in the late afternoon light, looking out at the enormous hedge. Whatever life held for him, whatever *waited* for him, lay beyond it now. There was an immense stillness, a perfect quietness to the tiny leaves. He had learned some French in this town, some other things. Well, it would pass. Time itself would pass.

Passion was some function of time.

DEATH OF A STREET DOG

The humans are watching me. They have noticed me because I couldn't decide which corner to go to. Midway across the street, I changed my mind, then changed my mind again. They have noticed I have no collar and that there is hair missing from my shoulder. If I don't keep moving now, they will call the chamber. They have noticed me now, all of them. But not in a good way. This is no time for an interview. I was undecided because every direction looked the same to me. Because all directions *are* the same to me. They are all downhill.

I'm too weak anymore; I'm too weak; but I could once walk on my hind legs, alone, for fourteen steps, standing up, like a human or a bear. That would be almost enough to cross this street. Not every dog can do that. Not every human or *bear* can do that. I am moving fast, now, as though I have someplace to go. I pass the real-estate office again and the picture of the little girls. Those girls could save me, I think, but I can't look at them at the moment. I go four blocks quickly, walking with my shoulders drooped. This calls too much attention to me, I know, but I can't hold them straight anymore. I could wag my tail but I'd better not. Wagging my tail scares people away. Two alleys, three, then right. I know where there is a house with an add-on at the back. I can see in three directions from there, from near the toilet pipe. I have been there before. I will go now if no one follows.

I tried an interview this morning. I failed my interview. I lie down and wait under the add-on. Wait and wait. How many minutes? A long time. Should I try to sleep? No. Better not. I hear someone calling a dog.

Not me.

But it *is* me. Doggie! they are saying.

Then I hear it.

Pinga-pinga-pinga-pinga-pinga.

The high note from the exhaust of the van from the chamber! A sharp up and a slight down noise. Ping-a. Ping-a. Absolutely unmistakable.

The humans have called the chamber on me!

I hear the van a full block away, then half a block away, then coming down the alley. PINGA-PINGA-PINGA-PINGA. Did someone see me duck under? I bury my chin in the grey dirt near the toilet pipe. The noise goes steadily past. Then it is going away, two blocks, then three.

Much fainter now: pinga-pinga-pinga-pinga-pinga.

Doggie! they are saying. But that is not my name.

Actually, I don't think I have a name anymore. I once had a name. What was my name? Buddy? I had the name Buddy once. Or Buster. Something like that. I came to it. Weeks and weeks, months and months ago, more than a year now. I had humans then. I did not fail my humans. We lived in a little silver trailer in a little silver trailer park. A boy and his father. We would watch TV together. The boy would get spankings and I would put my paws on his thigh. Day after day, night after night. The boy would cry and hold me. Sometimes, that is. Sometimes he would do neither. My paws on his thigh. It was the boy that taught me all the tricks. I wonder what became of him? There was a day when the father took me for a long drive in the woods. He let me out and pushed me away from the car. I thought it was a game. I thought he wanted to see if I could find my way back home all by myself. I *did* find my way back all by myself! It took me a day and a half, almost two full days. I was so proud of myself! When I got there, it was exactly the same place, I knew. The tree. The mailbox. But the trailer was gone. There was some sand and high grass where it had been, but the trailer itself was gone. I came back every day for four months but the trailer stayed gone. So did the boy. People began chasing me then because I was beginning to look bad. Then I quit coming back. I thought it was a game. I did not fail my humans. My humans failed me.

I think it is safe to leave from under the house now.

(Still, I wait another long time before actually leaving.)

Girls, though. I don't think human girls would have let that happen. There are two girls on a picture at the real-estate agency, a house with a porch, little girls, both waving. I think they are the children of someone who works there. I thought about following the people home but there are too many of them and they get in cars. Little girls are good to work for, at least from what I can see. They might live right here in town. I think they do. A porch railing. A window. A certain style. I've looked and looked for it. I think it is here, though. If only I could find the girls. I have the strongest sense that they are waiting for me. I can't explain it. It's one of those odd things, like a fruit, but different.

I am away from the add-on now. I made it away safely. The first move from or to a place is always the most dangerous. But I stumbled, got sick and threw up in the street and called attention to myself. It will be getting dark soon. I can't make it back to my field tonight. But that was the decision I made before I left. I must remind myself, that was the decision. My field is not really a big field. It has a ditch in it and a little cave-like area that some kids made, a kind of fort, they would call it. That's what the boy called it when he made it. "This is our fort," he would say. But kids don't use it anymore. I've never seen even one there.

real little girls, a real house, somewhere in town. I have tricks I know that I could show them. I know how to drop a ball close to feet and shoes, so that it can be thrown easily again by the humans. (Some dogs never understand that.) I can walk upright, as I've said. I can chase what they call a Frisbee and catch it in midair. Bubbles too. If someone blows soap bubbles I can pop them with my nose before they hit the ground. But no one is going to blow bubbles for me anymore. Not with these ulcers. These ulcers are getting worse every day, much worse. I can't interview much longer. I may not be able to interview now. I don't want to think about it. I won't be able to say tomorrow much longer. Everything that tomorrow means, I won't be able to say. Maybe I can't even say it today. Tomorrow means that you are giving time a chance. When you have to say today, you are pressing against time, begging it. There is something impolite about it. When you have to say today, the world is an entirely different place, an entirely different *kind* of place.

It is not true, though, anyway, and it's never been true, that the field is perfectly safe. Three times they have sent the van there for me. The men in the van don't get far from roads. Here dog! Here doggie! they say. Pinga-pinga-pinga in the background. They have food, sometimes. Once, they came out into the field itself after me. They had not seen me, or at least I don't think they had. They were just guessing. I watched them from deep inside the fort. They had a flashlight and a long fishing pole. With the pole, they raised a croker sack nailed up by some now-grown kid. They raised it and shined the flashlight slowly back and forth. But I know better than to be in a straight line from the entrance. Slowly, very slowly, they flashed around with the light, the van still running in the distance. Then they left.

I am here, now, on the sidewalk, because I have to gamble. I must remind myself, always; I have to go farther than ever. I have to say today. Already this is a neighborhood I have never been in. The houses are different, too. Houses are not alive, but they come in types, like birds; similar houses flock together. I have never really understood why that is. Up, down, up, and down the blocks. As fast as I can. But I can't go very fast. Down, up, down, across. Then across again. I see a railing like the porch railing in the picture. But the windows are different. Then there is a window like but with a different railing.

I am seeing no *people*, though. Every place I look, I am seeing no one. Then I do. An elderly lady, raking her lawn. The railing is exactly like the one in the real-estate picture! She might be the grandmother of the girls! I wag my tail until I see that she has noticed me. She is holding very tightly to her rake, now. I must not step on her lawn. She is holding very, very tightly to her rake, backing away now, keeping her rake between us. I know what she is going to do. She is going inside to phone. I must visibly hurry away. (Am I running fast enough for you lady?) Here dog! Here doggie! they say in their gentle, baby-like voices. I guess some dogs must come. They have some food sometimes. I've often wondered whether or not it is poisoned.

I go two more blocks then quickly along a long iron fence. Before I turn the corner, I see a gap in the leaves and stop to look through the gap. Why did I do that? Why on *earth* did I do that? What I saw was the *van*! Parked, its engine stopped! No pinga-pinga! Three more feet and I would have been visible! Never twice in one day have they called the *van* on me! I must be looking very bad.

(How could they possibly know where I am? How could they get here so soon? Is it possible to phone to a *car*?)

But there is a culvert halfway down the block, and no one looking on this street. I could sleep in the culvert. They won't dream a dog would sleep in a culvert, especially while it's still light. No dog in its right mind would sleep in a culvert, light or *no* light. I am so exhausted now. I stoop down and begin to crawl inside. My ulcer is scraping against the roof. Careful, very careful. The culvert is not big, not long either. It only goes under a little side street. I must force myself to smell around very carefully. Everything is OK. As long as it doesn't rain. It smells very bad but I am so exhausted. I cannot ev— No! No! Oh my *God*! There is a *snake!* A *snake*! A snake right here in the culvert! I didn't even *smell* her! I can see her now. And her babies, fresh-born with egg shells. She's rattling her tail near the other end. Not far, but near the other end. That's how sick I am! That's how sick I am and how my nose is not working! There is no place else to go, though. Be *quiet*, snake! The van will *hear* you! They'll kill you *too*! Just for the fun of it! Listen to me! She is rattling, seconds and seconds, rattling while I watch her silvery eyes. If she stays at her end... (Rattling, but quieter now, then quieter still, now completely quiet, not moving.) Still looking, though. No more than twenty feet away. If she stays at her end... If all her babies stay at their end... If there is nothing else crawling my way. With certain sorts of animals there can be a truce for sleep and water. I don't know about snakes. A snake is an uncertain sort of animal. But she is not moving anymore. Let me lie down. Let. Me. Lie. Down. Now?

Did I sleep? Sleep full of worry is not sleep. Sleep full of worry has no rest in it. That is wisdom. Without humans, I have accumulated wisdoms. I am dying of accumulated wisdoms. Did I sleep again? There are ants crawling all over my ulcers now. I lick and bite them away. There are some I can't get to, tunneling into it. I...

It is before dawn when I wake for the last time. The snake has not moved. All night long, she has been coiled like a garden hose, watching me, protecting her cylindrical babies. I crawl out of the culvert and look. The van is gone. I begin again, quickly, going through street after street. Up and down, looking for the girls. My paws are sore. But this is the safest time. What I discover, though, when I look at the sun when it rises is that it's not tomorrow, despite the long night. It is *still* not tomorrow. What it is is today again. Today.

I have not been in this area before. I can't be predictable. I must cover all the streets and sidewalks without being predictable. I must hurry now, before many people are awake. My left front paw is beginning to bleed.

I go for miles and miles, walking, walking. Even with my limp, I have covered miles, I know. I had no idea the town would go on and on. I thought it was a small town. I have always heard this referred to as a small town, a small *country* town. But I don't know exactly what a country is. I know there is a country *road* somewhere with a house on it where they shoot dogs and feed them to pigs and videotape them being eaten. (Alive, that is; the dogs are still alive.) I thought country might mean something like small. But this country *town* goes on and on, street after street, house after house, with more people awake now, with more and more cars moving. I am so sick from that rabbit. I thought I needed the meat. I thought the meat would be good for me.

Down a long, long street. Down another. Quickly—or as quickly as I can—with more and more people awake. Any person who sees me, notices me. No person sees me without noticing me now. I must not wag my tail; wagging my tail scares people away. Please tell me what I'm supposed to do when wagging my tail scares people away?

I don't know what happened to lead to all this. Maybe I had a false pride. Maybe I displeased the boy and his father. Maybe the father got jealous of my abilities. Maybe no one wants a dog that can walk on his hind legs.

I was attacked by a much larger dog and a lot of my hair is missing. That's exactly why I was attacked, too. I tried to stand up. I was trying to show off so the humans could see me. I thought it might work. There was a crowd, a lot of humans, several dogs. I thought it was worth a try. I was attacked by the largest dog before I had taken four steps. Maybe what I can do is nothing. Maybe it is not enough. Maybe there is something I am doing wrong. I say I can walk fourteen steps on my hind legs. But that was really the best time, ever. I may be bragging about it too much. Nothing else ever came close to that. That may be why I lost my humans. Even with the Frisbee and the bubbles. Sometimes they hit the ground.

The houses are really getting big and fancy in this area. There are huge oak trees along the streets, sprinklers too. Unlike houses, sprinklers can be a little bit alive. They don't *smell* alive so I didn't believe it when I first heard. I laughed about it, in fact. (I mean, you know, the way dogs laugh.) But then one afternoon, I saw it for myself. I saw a sprinkler crawl the full length of a lawn.

The porch railing on that house is very like. But the window is wrong. Next door to that, though. (Would you *look* at the house next door to that!) I've never in my life seen such a house! The lawn, too. There is an iron fence around it. It's like a dream. No such places are real.

Look! There are dogs also! Two of them! *Girl* dogs in the yard! The type the humans call Cocker Spaniels!

They have seen me! Look! They are coming the full length of the yard to see me! I cannot believe this is happening! They are coming to talk to *me*! Maybe that's what the picture meant! *Dog* girls not human girls! Maybe the picture meant *dog* girls! Society types!

(I put my nose though the iron bars.)

Maybe if they like me I'll be invited in! Maybe if their humans see us talking! This could be like an interview! I can't believe what is happening! They have *ribbons* in their hair!

No. They turned. They were being called by an opened door. I really don't believe they saw me.

Anyway, their humans might not have let them talk to me. My "kind," they might have said, my "kind."

What is my kind, exactly? My kind is a kind that can walk fourteen steps on his back legs without falling. My kind is a kind that knows how to drop the ball at the humans' feet so it can be thrown again. My kind is a kind that can pop bubbles and pop every bubble before it hits the ground. My kind is a kind without luck.

(My kind is also a kind that will brag even in the midst of despair.)

My left paw is beginning to bleed again. Why am I doing this? My life has become one long day. I may be clinging to a torture. It may not be so bad to quit. My mother knows. All my brothers and sisters know. How bad could it be? My biggest lack may be a lack of imagination.

I look at the lawns and sprinklers. I stop near a very small sprinkler, turning and turning in front of me. I would give anything to go on the lawn under that sprinkler. That little sprinkler on its very own lawn! But they would call the chamber on me.

Look! Look!

Without the sprinkler, I wouldn't have *seen* it! On the side block! Right there! It's the *house*! The girls too and their father! They're on the lawn! Right now! Right here! There they are! There father is sweeping the sidewalk! I can't *believe* it!

(I did it! I *did* it! I can't stand it! I held on! I did it! They're only fifty feet away!) My heart is beating so fast I can't stand it! I need to stop and compose myself. I need to slow down. They haven't seen me yet.

Careful. I must approach them carefully and gently. I must remind myself, this is the most important interview of my life. I must compose myself. My knees are shaking. I must be sure to go to the older sister first. Very tiny girls can be afraid of dogs. The older girl now. Careful, keep your nose down. But be sure you look at each one equally when they turn. Wag your tail just a little bit, but keep it down, low, so they can't see it much. (Careful, careful.) Don't frighten her. She hasn't seen you yet. (I held on! I held *on*. I *did* it! *No* dog could have done what I did!)

But it's not over yet. Careful. Don't frighten her. See! She is seeing you now. Don't be too shy, look up at her. Look! she's starting to *smile*!

What's going on? Something's going wrong. What? What? Her smile is pulling way too wide. She's beginning to cry. She's crying now. She's yelling for her father!

"Daddy! He's ugly! He's *ugly*! Make him go *away!*"

A stick! A stick in the ribs! Give me a stick in the ribs! Yes sir! You brave man! You brave and well-fed man!

I cannot tell you what happened after that. Miles and miles I may have gone. This way and that. I almost got run over twice, by two separate cars. One of the cars left long skid marks for foot after foot on the asphalt road. I became so lost, all because of that man with his stick. But for months and months every one of my hopes and dreams had been wrapped up in those two little faces and I saw them go like bubbles popping.

Finally, I found myself on a road of gravel, which later turned into a road of dirt. I had seen a road of gravel before, once. But never in my life had I seen a road of *dirt*. Such a strange thing to see. Almost unbelievable. Can *cars* go down it?

Staggering along in the dirt itself, I see that there are no garbage bins now, no dumpsters, no familiar smells. The houses are spread much wider apart. Many of them are ugly. Some are unpainted, with plywood nailed to them in places. There are abandoned cars in some of the yards. There is some laundry hanging from poles and wires. I see a house with some chickens behind it.

(There are low clouds, too, above the road. The clouds don't look encouraging to me.)

I am so sick. Rabbit, why couldn't you have died later? You weak little rabbit, with your big weak eyes. It's not supposed to be this way between us. You had been dead too long, your roundness was gone. You were flat like the earth.

Each step I take now is a perfect agony. I see these low clouds and this life, this damned life, this damned God who laughs at me. Why did I leave my field? There was always food there from the pizza parlor. Maybe the ulcers would have healed on their own. Maybe I gave up too soon. After all, I had the fort and the shopping center. It was a life. Why did I have to gamble it? I am so lost, so weak, too weak to think. But all of that is uphill and behind me now and I can't go uphill.

Suddenly, I trip and fall flat, completely sprawl out in the hot dirt. In trying to right myself, I mess on myself then I realize my legs are not working properly. I have to drag them. I can't use my *legs*! I can't use my *legs*! I pull myself forward with my front paws for several steps: four, five, six, seven, eight... No. Suddenly my legs are working again. Wonder what that was all about?

What keeps things alive. Hearts? Humans say hearts. But some say other things. Some say oats, some say grain, some say meat, some say fish. But hearts, the humans say. So stop heart, I say. But it doesn't stop. And what do I do now? I took a wrong turn or ten wrong turns. It was that man with the stick, the father of the little bubbles. I am so lost. There is no hope for me anymore. But I don't want hope. I want nothing to do with hope. What I want is *luck*. Hope can kill you.

I am beyond tired now. I am beyond exhausted. I am walking downhill. But without this downhill slope I could not be walking at all. (There is something very strange indeed about these clouds, which are getting ever lower.) Step after bleeding step, I take. I have done all I can do in life and it has not been enough. I have done each and every thing I can and all I can, and *more* than I can, and it has not been enough and it will not *be* enough. I see that now. It is all so useless without luck—without luck meeting you halfway, or part of the way or coming the smallest fraction of an inch in your direction. And I have had no luck, no luck whatsoever. It is a dirt road, a very strange and curious dirt road I am on. So be it. I shall move to the very center of this road. I shall let the whole world see me, let the van swoop down on me from behind.

I shall not hide anymore: call me doggie, then; I will come; I will eat your food.

But the van comes not and I pass yard after yard, ugly house after ugly house. I go through time and more time. Slowly, too, I begin to realize what I am seeing in the clouds. It is the shadows of dogs, of millions of dogs, of an infinite number of dogs. I hear their voices calling me everywhere, reflected even from the moon. I join a procession stretching through all time. I hear the endless whispering of uncountable voices, from the sharpest yap, to the longest, loudest baying. I feel the slapping sting of tails, the endless breath of pantings, the thrill of the hunt, the tug and pull of puppies, their little bites, their little licks and squirmings. Other things, too, I see, feel, hear, and smell, good things, tales of blood and urine, half-remembered things that I cannot begin to describe, nothing odd in any of it, either, nothing like a *fruit* to distract me now. Am I dying? I must be dying to see such visions.

But around me, still, on the road I feel that I am seeing well. The houses are thinning rapidly. There is only a section of field now and one last house that swims in the heat of distance. Who knows how far I've gone? Who can measure such distances?

Suddenly, all the visions fade, because, dying or not (and perhaps I'm not really dying) I have come to the end of the road. Very literally, the road ends here. There is the one lone house and a turn-around area for cars, a very strange and odd-looking little house that I stagger toward steadily. Is this the house of the videos? But I think there are men in that house, men or boys, or both. And what I see now is a woman.

In any case, I have not the strength to turn around.

I have no choice. I shall come to a full stop in your yard, Mrs. Woman. I can see you are horrified. Run inside then. Phone the chamber. Better yet, go and get your husband. Tell him to bring his shotgun. What I need is an instrument of destruction.

(There is a chicken-wire fence. I see some animals watching me through it.)

The woman is a tiny doll in the heat of my vision.

Why is no one moving? Time is spreading around me now, like a spreading pool of blood. Is it a second or several minutes that I have been standing here?

The animals are looking at me, at my ulcers and fur.

They are all watching me, as still as paintings on the cloudy sky. I am struggling. I lock my knees in order to stand before them. It was that rabbit, that damned weak rabbit. What was she doing there?

They are still watching. What is this all about? Why won't this moment come to an end?

Through the chicken wire, I can see a half-acre of land, a tiny windmill, a pond, a one-legged duck, a one-eyed tomcat, three girls not one of them society types. I don't know what it means. What could it possibly mean? All the other houses were ugly but this one is neat and clean. It could mean *luck* and the end, the death, of my life on the street. It could mean something else. I'm too sick to think about it at the moment. It is entirely too distant to be of concern. I am collapsing, right now, in front of all of them. Still, if it *does* mean something else, so be it. I am without fear in the matter.

I am without fear for all time.

I shall die like a dog, not a human.

L' ANNONCIATION
(The Story of m.)

I'm in trouble with m. I have slapped her without her permission. As much as m. loves to be slapped, the distinction is problematic if not theoretical. Still, when she looks at me now, her eyes are burning with a new kind of fire.

I suppose I won't be at m.'s house for a while—though truly I am not often there when she is with another man. (And this, despite the fact that she very much prefers me to be around.) m. is afraid something might happen to her, and, of course, something might. If things get out of control I know where the gun is. Most often, though, it is m. that gets out of control. What she does not realize, is that I am prepared to shoot her as well.

I cannot say that things have been going satisfactorily lately. I am emotionally shot. I am drained and exhausted. I am living a grey life. I am possibly dead. (m. may be dead as well.) My heart continues to beat, though, from habit or inertia. I continue to watch the world, on occasion, to act. Sometimes, when I think about it, I take a breath.

I am more than upset that I have slapped her.

I remember, years ago, during an excessively hypothetical time of my life, a discussion with a graduate-student girlfriend of the kind of things m. is into. I don't remember exactly how the subject came up. (How do these things ever come up?) The girl said she was not interested in such things herself but saw no problem with two consenting adults under the influence of an uncontrollable passion.

What did I think?

Quite truthfully, I did not know what I thought. I wasn't sure there were any such things as adults, much less consent.

We started across a footbridge and I tossed over two rocks:

I was afraid these might be two consenting rocks under the influence of an uncontrollable gravity.

In her defense, m. would not say anything so stupid.

m. of course, would not say anything at all.

In her bedroom there are numerous small pools of wax and the remains of candles on all the level surfaces...

It probably doesn't matter that we are not speaking; m. and I have nothing to talk about. When we are together we are immersed in a great silence. Years ago, we had something that passed for affection. But now she merely disturbs an endless dialog I have with myself. I am more alone with her than without her.

In truth, I prefer to be out of her presence.

When we are talking of m. and myself, we are talking neither love nor hate nor friendship nor apathy. We are talking a relationship that simply cannot be defined. m. is not what I want and I am not what she wants. There is truly only one perdurable thing between us: a sort of understanding.

m. says, or might say: "We waste our time together."

I might answer, I know.

—Why do we bother?

—I don't know.

—Should we quit seeing each other?

—Yes.
—Will we?
—Yes.
—Will we really?
—No.
Either of us can recite either half of the conversation.

m. and I are not married, nor have we ever been. In fact,
a husband would get in m.'s way. She has made close to
three million dollars in stocks and bonds. I believe she made
over a hundred thousand in commodities in the last four
months. m. doesn't work at all. She makes telephone calls.
She looks at her computer screen. She drinks and fucks.
    In truth, she has too much time.
    m. is not malicious, though, not evil either, by and large,
though she looks at the numbers on her computer screen
with ice-cold eyes. I would not like to be a number on that
screen. About the other, she is blasé. "Try not to care so
much," she says. "It's all fakery anyway."
    This is what she says.
    She lies, though (of course).
    Passive as a cow, m. is, at times, though she is capable of
being the definitive woman. What she is not capable of is
being unattractive, which is exactly the problem. The word
she chooses for me to try not to...*care*...is interesting.
Actually, I don't think that word has any meaning for me.
    —Besides, she says, you don't even like me. I'm just a
curiosity for you, like a two-headed cat.
    —Perhaps. A cat though... I'm not so sure. I'm not really
that fond of cats.

There is something almost frantic about m's sexuality. No
sooner does she have a man in her than she wants him out
again, than she wants his sex pounded and drained into her,
than she wants another one. What she loves is the conquest,
the anticipation, the first introduction and porcelain
shouldering into whatever is the most convenient orifice.

She devours these cock-things like a fat boy eating hot dogs—and with the same appetite.

Or like someone sucking the juice from plums.

What she seems to want forever is the strange face, the strange mouth, the strange genitals, steaming, hot from the fly. The screwing itself apparently wastes her time. (Confinement, though, she likes; and, if you untie her, she will cry.) She becomes like a child at Christmas, unwrapping gifts, tugging on zippers or belts; or like a cat: licking, nibbling. Is it pierced, tattooed, circumcised? Does it have a purple head? Can she make it grow? Can she make it grow *fast*? This is her animal, her pet.

Otherwise, I'm not sure what it is, exactly.

One might say m. is in one of the traps life prepares for the oversophisticated woman.

One would be wrong, though.

m. is bright, but knows nothing, actively rejects all forms of knowledge. *Wisdom* is what she rejects most viscerally. You can't discuss anything with her; she will squirm away or kiss you to shut you up. Nevertheless, occasionally, with m., you will find you have had a most profound conversation. The difference is: you are never working from the fruits of culture, but from first principles.

You might be in the South Seas in the time of Cook or Melville.

m. might be a native who has removed her grass skirt.

She is living in a slower time at a faster pace. I'm not sure that it is possible to be jealous of her if you know her really well. Jealously requires a more complex reference system. I am *some*thing, no doubt, but jealous is not the word.

The truth is I have pimped her once—not for money, or any voyeur streak, which in fact is nonexistent in me, but because she has, on occasion, asked me to, as often as four times a night. I finally gave up, or in.

Actually, I don't think I was much help. She more or less got the guy herself, a virtual skinhead with prominent temporal veins. I think I was using that logic of the homeopathic magic: a man who looks like a cock should be able to perform like one. Actually, he had not managed to get the condom on before...well, before things happened that made it superfluous.

m. was not amused.

I waited till the man was gone then seduced (fucked would be her term) her myself. She became tender then, girl-like, babbling romantically. We were in cahoots. But I was not fooled. This guy was not a success. She wants five more.

I have carte blanche at m.'s house: a white card—or map (or what is the other, not exactly similar thing: a tabula rasa). Still, I prefer not to watch when she is with another man, though I once had a vague idea I might discover some enjoyment in engineering her orgasms. I walked barefooted into her bedroom. To my surprise, they were on the floor. The guy had a homemade tattoo on his left buttock. Above that was what looked like an abscess. His rectum seemed excessively loose and puckered as though something large had torn it, which is probably the case. I could see, momentarily, a thick segment of his *turgidity*, moving in and out of her, looking vaguely milky in its condom.

I stood there a moment.

No, I thought.

(Actually, I felt he was doing a better job than I could.)

m. was in another world, sucking like a blind puppy; then her eyes were open, looking through me. Her beauty will simply not go away. Our pupils did not even begin to do what one could call meeting.

I walked out again.

In separate chairs, sometimes, we sit, side by side, and dream of separate people, or how we might redesign one another. Of what legitimacy is the body as pure sculpture for the uses of desire? I think of the barnyard: the cows, the pigs, the chickens, the sheep and goats and how irrelevant to what is turned into food is personality.

(Personality.)

With m. all education, all life, all lessons of all types, all of the tempering of hopes and fears are subsidiary to the growing of firm breasts and genitalia. Humans could be aged in a room or turned on *spits* in the sun; they could be displayed live in those huge European markets near the lobsters and tuna. We are not talking thoughts or talents; we are not talking *any*thing; we are talking a warm body and pure drive or supplication. We are talking the minimum that God himself might *deign* to be worshiped by.

God himself, I say.

m. is not at all athletic. She is uncoordinated with that super-feminine and spastic *un*-coordination which is both utterly stereotyped and familiar. You want to laugh out loud. Then suddenly she will roll you over and more or less screw you with your own cock, drive into your groin with a strength and persistence that is frightening. She gets what she wants. It is not you; it is not *it*; it is not *any*thing; yet she gets it, I say. She is attracted to beauty, to women, to long-maned men with eyes like horses. But that's an early stage. When she is on fire, she is attracted to anything. There is a space in her bed for even the deformed and hideous. It is the fascination, perhaps, of the whole for the damaged flesh. What is more interesting is how the purely selfish, the *perfectly* selfish, can become paradoxically generous and embracing—how one can approach what are advertised as Christian parameters from a dark or evil side.

Blessed art thou among women, m. Sort of.

God himself, I say. (Or Mary, mother of God.)

I remember once almost stumbling upon an elderly man who was entwined with m. on a rug. I was surprised to see them in this particular room. I honestly didn't know they were there. I was simply on my way to the refrigerator. For a moment, I didn't know what I was seeing. (There is a level at which I *still* don't know.)

The man became anxious and frightened when he saw me.

"Don't worry," m. said, pulling him down and kissing him passionately. "I'm very serious. You are safe." She explored with her tongue, the recesses of his soul. (This, no doubt, for my benefit.)

"Yes," I said, "pay no attention to the man behind the curtain."

But my presence had changed the situation in a way he didn't like. Of course, I could have said something very similar about him or a hundred others. I went back and stayed in the living room until they were finished.

Later, in an attempt to salvage some dignity, the man (after all, I'd seen his buttocks and rectum prior to his face) took a moment to speak to me. He was taller than I, and, fully dressed, looked almost senatorial, even something like a movie star. Obviously he was not used to being compromised in such a fashion.

m.'s living room was a complete mess. The man stood there and deliberately took all of it in: the beer cans, the cigarettes, the whiskey bottles, the trays full of ashes, the mirror lying flat on a chest, the music videos on a small TV rolling slowly out of sync. "I thank God (he said) I'm not young in so thoroughly finished a world."

I nodded and let him out.

But m. had heard us talking:

"What did he say?" she asked.

"He said he had a nice time. Is he a professor or something?"

"I think so. How did you know?"

"He plagiarized a line from Goethe."

m. was in bed now, wearing an almost formal, high-necked, nightgown, her long hair framing her face with the innocence of a Victorian school girl. She was wiping at something underneath the covers with a tissue.

Then she looked up and smiled.

*   *   *

The next morning I watched as m. worked in her flower garden. All symmetry and bright competitive colors, this is, lined on every side with bricks and pansies. When fully in bloom, it has an overwhelming, almost explosive sort of beauty and m. has a pride in it that will just about break your heart.

m. was working barefooted, listening to a cassette of Schubert's *E. Flat Mass* which I think I may have given her, patting the damp dirt into place with her toes. A necklace I had never seen before was dangling from her neck. I cannot begin to keep track of her gifts—trinkets, they are, for the most part and I don't know what she does with them all. What she wants, though, is not a trinket but a child.

(Actually, what she *wants* varies enormously from day to day.)

Over time, one learns to watch her eyes; they give the earliest signs of the changes coming. But watching m.'s eyes might very well challenge a naturalist. What you soon realize is there is no such thing as an acquaintance. Any man she makes significant visual contact with she has been with the night before, or last week, or will come back to find tomorrow. One appreciates how little all denials of affection mean (or can mean) for human beings who have been together physically. Her eyes will sweep and search then lock, drift, and lock again. Her attempts at a poker-face will dissolve into blushes and smiles. In a less public forum, something entirely different may happen. You really don't want to see that transition.

Nor do you want to slip on the puddles of wax on her floor.

It is not pleasure, particularly, that drives Miss m; there is no room for pleasure in her life; she can't get free of desire. On occasion, she will curl into my arms and cry all night, so miserable and afraid of what is happening to her. Then the next evening she will go out and do it all again.

(She has always been a girl to throw up in order to keep drinking.)

Nor must one discount the purely manipulative:

"You don't fuck me as often as you could," she once said, nuzzling close beside me.

—I know.

—How often would you fuck me if you really loved me?

—If I really loved you?

—If you really, really...

—That's easy, I say, pulling her smooth belly closer, but I'm surprised you ask.

—Well?

—Never.

Why, one might legitimately ask, do I even stay around?

Actually, my proximity is an illusion. There is a level at which I abandoned her years ago. There is another level at which I do not leave because I'm afraid I might miss something. The relationship is not nearly as one-sided as it may sound. m. is more than anxious to return all favors, always picking out women for me. (Wouldn't you like her? I could get her for you.) She can, too—and I'm not at all handsome—though the truth is she wants them for herself: their soft lips, their little waists.

Such gifts are too tempting and unfair, unfair even to offer. I seem to be paralyzed because of them, stuporous might be the better word.

m. is young but not *that* young, which is part of the problem. She is steadily approaching last-call, that point where she must drink up and leave the party. There is a sweatiness to her, a fatigue of the flesh, a smell of menstrual blood and stale perfume. In a bath, she does not come perfectly clean. She is wild at night but every morning checks her face almost gently in the mirror. Indeed, it may not be the female but the earth itself that is desperate.

She reminds me of an anxious swan streaming through dark and swampy water.

Not long ago, she found a baby bird in her garden and began feeding it daily with grubs. Soon, she had pinned all

her hopes on its tiny wings. I was just sick with worry.
Something purely good needs to happen to m. by day and
away from lust and alcohol. I just knew the bird would die.
(These things always die.) But it did *not* die in her care. She
bought a large Chinese cage for it with thin strips of wood,
darkly varnished. When he first flitted to a perch inside it,
she went into an ecstasy that was embarrassing to watch.

On the sofa, later, she placed her head in my lap. "What's
happening to me? I didn't have to turn out this way. It
didn't have to turn out this way, did it?"

"Probably not," I said (though I was more or less certain
I was lying).

Following such a comment, did I expect her to change, to
find everything has been a big mistake?

No.

What could I or anyone say that has not been said by
others for centuries if not millennia. I smoothed her long
hair and stayed silent. Indeed, m. was recovering already.
Her doubts ended with a sniff and a smile.

"I was always different," she said.

Perhaps because of the bird, I gave in recently on the
trapeze. (We have not mentioned this.) You see, its not just
a child that m. wants, but a trapeze. Yes, indeed, exactly
... and for exactly you know what.

m. and I were at the hardware store, buying pulleys,
cables, dowels and a winch. I designed it so it was way
overbuilt; one should not like to break her little neck
unintentionally. The salesclerk's name (Bob) was stenciled
in red in an oval on his shirt.

"Approximately how much do you need to lift?" he said.

"A hundred and twelve pounds," I answered.

A sudden wonderful smile from m., a curious look, too,
from Bob, who cannot bring himself to realize that what he
most desires to believe is true. The bill came to $83.45 and I
put it on a Visa. Of course, as I should have known, the
leather attachments for the hands (or feet) m. already had.

Later, working at her house, I became covered in sawdust and grit. It was a mess, a perfect pain in the ass, surely one can order such contraptions complete. But I'm not so sure that I would want to be on such mailing lists—not sure what other lists I may already have entered.

m. of course was hot to try it immediately. She had been drinking as I worked and already had a significant buzz on. I finished by drilling two holes though the ceiling and securing the pulley to a beam in the attic.

I winched her up, upside-down, and fully clothed. This had the unpleasant effect of aging her ten years. Then I lowered her so that her fingertips were just resting on the floor. She began giggling and grabbed at the bed. Her face had become purple and demonic. (Now, I thought, is my chance to leave her. *Now*, while I have no illusions.)

"Come on," she said, starting the trapeze swinging. "Lock the doors. I am yours to play with. What's a little blood between friends?"

Very interesting. Do you understand what she has just said?

No, I guess it would be doubly impossible to know.

(m. ran with her hands across the floor, setting the trapeze arcing higher and higher.)

Let me explain; m. was not on her period; this was her way of telling me I have not been hitting her hard enough. She wants the belts like lightning through her body. For the moment, I watched the cable and her head, moving together like a pendulum. She seemed to be marking time with her face. I'd already begun to repent of what I'd done. I scarcely dared to make sex any more of a game for her. She will fuck herself to death. There will be nothing left. I will come in some afternoon and find two consenting arms dangling from a trapeze.

m. doesn't trust me—completely, that is; she feels I am capable of anything and is more right than wrong. I suppose

I give her what she most wants which is pain and rejection. But I give her less of both than I used to. Why should I want her, though? She doesn't exist for me. More correctly, she does not exist for me any more than she exists for anyone else. I will simply not chase a mirage. Were I an Arab, I might well die a hundred yards from a very real oasis in order to avoid this chasing of mirages.

When I did begin to hit her harder, I became aware of the aesthetics of damage to her body. She looked very good the way I had beat her: a fat lip and a purple eye with layered colors, like Japanese ink, near her eyelids. The only thing that might have looked better was raw blood. I'm not certain why I gave in; it was not just because of her desire for it or the pleasure it brought her, but to ease my own frustration at having to deal overlong with this soul of a stockbroker: this buy, sell, trade, fuck, stuff.

She had on her collar and I padlocked the chain to it.

Would she stay here?

She would.

(I am too polite. It disappoints her, I know.)

The chain is long enough for her to reach the tub and also (barely) the toilet. Feces is shit, how can anyone have a fascination with it?

There was evidently more room on that chain than I realized. When I returned in the afternoon, m. was on something; there was some alien substance, not alcohol, in her body. Her face looked blowzy; one could see in her eyes that her memory had receded to pinpoints. Her distant pupils seemed to rattle like craps in her brain. Her mouth was moving like a guppy's. She wanted a kiss on her smeared lips. How long can or will I kiss a woman who I know is not in love with me? The answer seems to be indefinitely. To what extent will the flesh work anyway? What is being offered and by whom? m. entered the world of sex prior to the advent of the viruses, but I think she misses the memory of that serum of old and would risk (or take) death in order to have it warm and wet inside her again.

Do you remember the high-school locker-room conversations, among sixteen-year-olds? The endless rhetorical questions:

What would you prefer to marry, a blonde or a brunette?

It wouldn't matter as long as she was a *nympho*maniac.

Ah...

A good thing to be, sixteen, I think.

m. is going to die soon; that is inevitable and I might as well admit it. She is not sick, or *known* to be sick, but what she is doing would kill anyone.

Tragic, I guess.

But then, too, she wants to die and has asked me more than once to kill her: "How?" I said, finally.

"Shoot me."

"Well?" I said.

m. didn't seem to understand.

"Give me the gun," I said.

m. got out of the bed, opened the nightstand and loaded her thirty-eight with six heavy bullets. Then she snapped the cylinder shut. On the ceiling, I watched the shadows of her body thrown by the night light. Her movement around the bed had released a wave of perfume in the room. She returned and handed it to me and settled in once more, laid her head on her pillow and smoothed her long dark hair around her ear.

I pressed the gun firmly to her temple. Then, with an oily click, I moved the chamber one position to the left. (I felt it was up to me, not chance, to select the bullet.) "You're sure about this?" I said.

She was, yes.

I got on my knees beside her in the bed.

Of course this would be the end of my life, too, but actually I was far more curious as to how much blood would come out, what her body would do, whether it would convulse or spasm, whether she might have time or

ability immediately afterwards to turn and look and realize
I had done it.
    (I also wondered how long it would take for the
neighbors and police to arrive.)
    "OK," I said. "Look at the clock. The time of this is very
important."
    Without raising her head, m. tilted it so I could see barely
her luminous eyes. I pressed the muzzle more firmly
against her temple.
    At that moment, she finally realized I was really going to
do it and grabbed my hand.
    "Fine," I said, "but always remember the time."
    Some months later, when m. was drunk (as always), I
quizzed her and found she had entirely forgotten not only
the time but, almost, believe it or not, the event.
    The exact moment of her near-death is evidently for me
alone to remember.
    The truth is, I should have expected it; this was a bit more
than a fact; it went beyond knowledge to revelation, almost
to wisdom, m. therefore rejects it. In such matters, it is
impossible to overestimate her stubbornness. I have an
image of her skull being entirely solid within and of a
uniform density of bone. In a graveyard I imagine seeing it
sliced or broken-open like a statue or Styrofoam ball. The
effect, I think, would be both eerie and frightening. People
look at m., now, and see what they most desire or fear.
    What they might see, then, is the extent of the deception.
    Though her body is wonderful, her face has undoubtedly
the greater reality. I expect it to be enduring through time,
like the face of a china doll. Her eyes are liquid and lively
but what consciousness she possesses is *there*, and not
elsewhere. One might be seeing not the eyes of a human
being at all but two very green and primitive creatures,
collaborating.
    Why did I slap her? What could possibly provoke it that I
haven't seen or heard a hundred times? The exact details are

unimportant. But the truth is this life of hers is not without its penalties. Something about m. that was once very large seems to have shrunk to the size of an insect. The empathy between us is largely the empathy of two creatures undergoing simultaneous destruction. But m. is somewhat ahead on the path. She seems to have broken free from the pain. m. has become like an annoying bee, getting ever louder, closer and more persistent. The interesting thing, as in the bee, just before it stings you seem to be able to *feel* it think.

I felt m. think and slapped her back to the stone age.

Where would she be now?

At the moment it is very late, or early…as you like it. m., of course, would not be alone. Quite likely, she is wearing a silk kimono but is otherwise nude, standing in her bedroom. Quite likely, she has lit a small candle. Quite likely, she has said, "I am yours for as long as this candle burns. Do anything you have ever wanted to do to a woman."

(The candles are not all that small, actually. They burn a good while.)

Has she actually said that to me?

Let us not dwell on the obvious.

Have I heard her say it to other men, or to other people, or to fair-sized groups of other people?

Let us simply not talk about it.

"Why?" she said to me once, crying, her pale skin half-covered with the very bruises that she herself had asked for.

"Because," I answered.

"Because why?"

"Because if you light a firecracker in a concert hall, the grand piano will hum."

"*What!?*" she said, suddenly laughing, smiling, trying to focus on my face. "Kiss me."

So we kissed and quit talking.

But truly there has not always been such a distinction between skin and nerve.

Pain and vision.

I did not add that, though. What I did was scratch her head.

What I said was, "Go to sleep."

What I pretended was that I didn't understand.

Not long ago, I visited a huge city where m. had once lived. I was passing through a district of seedy strip-joints on the way to a subway and found myself walking beside a group of slick promotional pictures—the type that are on glass or plastic and are lit from behind. (Which of course are never up-to-date and bear little relation to the women inside the clubs.) Suddenly I stopped. What I saw was totally unexpected. That's m! I thought, looking up. The eyes were absolutely unmistakable, also a slight lump, like a perpetual bruise on her lower lip. She looked demure, shy, excited. Was she flirting with the photographer? She seemed delighted with this dress with the white fur. I stood for a moment under the rolling lights. m. had looked much younger then; there was even an aspect of borrowed sexuality: a little girl all dressed up in her mother's tits. The bright lights seemed to add to a sense of silence and mystery. I have slept with this woman a thousand times and know nothing about her. This glass picture has been addressing every male that has stood on this sidewalk for a decade or more; nevertheless, there is something almost virginal about it: m's portrait could be in a cathedral and not look out of place.

I felt conspicuous and after a minute went on. Indeed, there was no need to stop any longer. m.'s picture was somewhat faded and I couldn't help but wonder why it had not been changed in all this time. There was no need to dwell on such things. Perhaps the purely masculine and purely feminine are but *zones* of life that the individual passes through. The truth is, if m. returned and stood beneath that marquee, I think she might well cry at seeing her younger self. The more interesting thing, though, is that the tears she would shed would be akin to those a man would shed for a woman.

* * *

Enough of this.

m. wants a child.

Well, there is time for that; and I've come to see that there may be something very like a sacrament in a child. It could be a moot point, though, since I happen to know, through an angel-like friend of hers, that m. has not bled in three months. m. is either damaged, then, or pregnant. The child, *if* a child, is always possibly mine, though with a woman who has intersected this many men it might as well be by God himself.

(God himself.)

I am not optimistic. Despite her condoms, m. will catch the disease of the times and it will kill her slowly. When her skin has grown thin and it is time for her to die, perhaps I should hasten the assumption, shoot her carefully if not gently in the head, then proceed with a series of shots spaced evenly along her cranium, like a halo. Indeed, it might be nice to get something into that thick skull of hers. But the truth is I would do this—and I *would* do this—out of neither malice nor pity.

(It would be more in the spirit of wrapping a corsage in tissue paper and putting it away before it dries completely.)

SAUTÉING THE PLATYGAST

At nightfall we lit a lantern to begin our search. We do better with lanterns; they give a quieter, gentler light; I am convinced that the filament of a flashlight makes a sound. (Not *much* of a sound, mind you, but there are creatures out there that can hear it.) We were in particularly fertile territory now, the wild thickets below the bog. Still, I had my doubts about this; we seldom hunt as a family and we were making altogether too much noise. The ground was dry; nevertheless, within a week of a rain can be a dangerous time to hunt. My son and daughter were carrying the torches as well as a broom and shovel. My wife was staying close to me in the circle of light from the lantern. The dog was making most of the racket, pulling the cart behind us with the washtubs. I felt a foreboding and misgiving about all of it. I listened to the cicadas, to the frogs, to the resin in the crackling flames. The children had gotten somewhat ahead of us and I found myself watching the interesting shadows they cast. My daughter, especially, likes to carry a torch. "You *like* carrying a torch!" I said to her when we caught up again. But she is at a sullen age and I received (and expected) no reply. Whether she understands me or not, I could not say.

In addition to the lantern, I had my Luger and the newly modified prong, on which I have welded a sharpened, vee-shaped block so it won't slide so much on the vertebrae. The pockets of my jacket were stuffed with the egg cases of some *Stelacens*, the tense embryos nestled like pearls in the leathery pouches. I shelled a few of them out with my thumb as I walked. They are good to snack on: slick, vaguely iridescent, mainly skull but soft. Eaten alive they are almost gummy; floated in cream they remind one of blueberries; but best of all is the way I had prepared them tonight: toasted slightly, with butter and salt, the skin dried close to the bone[1] and giving a nut-like flavor.

I looked up at the new moon, the narrow rim as fragile as ice in the night sky. Inauspicious, it seemed to me. This was not a good time to be moving about; the air itself seemed to be holding out on us. I thought of those millennia past when the planet was lonely and the bulk of life was large, of the incredible saurians rumbling through this landscape, huddled against the emptiness and stars. It was an agony then, perfectly terrifying to be alive. Years ago, I used to tell my students:

"When you think of a *Tyrannosaurus rex*, gentlemen, nineteen feet tall and eight tons in weight. Think bluff, gentlemen! Think bluff!"

My son had stopped now and raised his hand for silence. "Bring the lantern, Frank," he said. (My children call me Frank.) He had found the first one. Then I saw it, too, at ground level, the silver-red discs of its eyes reflecting.

*   *   *

What a night! We caught three washtubs full and afterward had to hurry home to put the corrugated covers on top of them. As the creatures around here warm up, they become more active and begin to gnaw and scratch at one another. In fact, we had hardly finished putting the covers in place when I began to hear their skins scraping against the galvanized zinc of the tubs.

Soon afterward, there was an intermittent fierce whacking (Whack! Whack! Whack!) from the third tub which left dents and protuberances in the metal that were sobering to look at. There is a slope behind the cabin and this particular tub suddenly began to nudge and slide down it. The animals seemed to be boiling inside. There was a great banging and rattling of the handles and I saw a couple of the smaller creatures slither out from under the corrugations of the tin. I shot twice with my Luger but missed both of them and watched their tails bumping out of the circle of light.

Then I tied the tub to a stake.

We have appetites, this family, but cook as fast as we could, we were four days getting to the third tub. I then found that we had made a terrible mistake. There was only one creature left inside, his body swollen like a tick, his skin so tight it seemed about to change color. He had evidently eaten every other animal. There was not one bone left, not one scrap of skin. He lifted his head toward us and opened his mouth wide. He had no shell but the way he maneuvered his body in rotation reminded me of a turtle.

I stuck the gig in and nudged him experimentally. He snapped the head of it clean off. (It was the old-style gig with the wooden handle.) Is this the whacker, I thought, or is this what ate the whacker?

I looked deep into his bloodshot and obdurate eyes. "Careful," I said.

The real tragedy was that we had not gotten a better look at the other animals inside. The wife took my place and kept the whacker distracted while I slipped around behind him. He moved forward slowly and pressed his claws against the metal. Then I managed to get him though the neck with the prong. I drove his throat against the wall of the tub and bent his head backwards over his spine. The pressure I was exerting began to smear his pig-like nose and awful wedge of a mouth. Then he twisted and began to buck on me. The wife stabilized him with another gig in the left leg while little-Frank ran to get the mallet. Meanwhile, I drove the prong steadily into his spinal column, the sweat plastering my shirt, my left arm beginning to spasm from the strain. Suddenly, the stake pulled loose and the tub began to slide on the smooth dirt. My great fear was that this guy might be able to jerk loose and flip out onto the ground. His huge mouth was open now and I could see his long recursive teeth and the glass-like ridge of his jaw.

"You're about to slip, Frank!" my son said.

He was right. Fortunately, this new prong won't slide. As I drove the final blows through the cord, the whacker's neck folded like a thick towel and he made a series of convulsive movements with his limbs. He seemed to smile at me upside down. It was perfectly obscene, this smile, more of a smirk I should say; it reminded me not so much of one of your standard animals, as one of those fat, triangular-headed kids that one sometimes sees in drugstores.

In hopes that he might have swallowed a few of the smaller creatures whole, we cut him open on the spot and turned his stomach inside out. But there was nothing identifiable inside, not a paw.

It was malicious the extent of this mastication.

We made haste to cook him immediately. Indeed, his eyes had scarcely glazed over when we began our prayers. Unfortunately, in our rush, we grabbed too small a pan and his legs, which overrode the rim, were charred rather badly in the flames.

Not bad, it was, this meat; and, despite some fibers, not really so tough either, a bit like pangolin or anteater. Unfortunately, my children are sloppy and stingy eaters. During the prayer itself my daughter grabbed all the claws.

"She got them last time!" little-Frank yelled. But before we could stop her, my daughter had put two of them in her mouth and was crunching them, bones and all. The others we could not pry out of her fingers. My wife said nothing but smiled with the corners of her eyes.

(It seems my daughter cannot get heavy enough to suit my wife.)

The problem with this "whacker"—a *Rhynochelon*, I ended up calling him—was that there was nothing appropriate to go with such a lean and fibrous meat. In addition, there wasn't nearly as much *to* him as one might have expected from the circumstances. At the end of the meal, none of us were truly full. What would have been nice would have been a skewer of scalatoids but I kept very quiet about that.

I watched as my daughter put her fork down and began looking at me from across the table. My wife and little-Frank soon did the same.

"How about a platter of *gills*?!" I said, getting up and taking my dishes to the sink. (*Scalatoids*, their eyes were saying and I didn't want to go through it again.)

My decision about the scalatoid matter is final, as far as I'm concerned—but the story, perhaps, bears repeating:

Scalatoids[2], though filling, are not really large. They are of a size with or perhaps slightly smaller than hedgehogs. Their appearance is considerably different, though. Looked at ventrally, they are very like platygasters (or platygasts as we call them, a very common little creature hereabouts) but the stomach is not nearly so flat and they are not as good for sautéing. I had given up cooking scalatoids years ago; there was far too much *fat* in the things which I found impossible to render out. But working secretly, and entirely on her own, my daughter discovered a way to prepare them. What she accomplished was a good deal more than a culinary miracle; it seemed to defy all reason. One afternoon, she allowed us to watch her at work. Even afterward, though, the mystery remained; there was no essential difference in her technique or spices. The difference in flavor was amazing.

(From the taste alone, I would have said it was a different animal.)

It took me some time to find out what she was doing. Scalatoids, you must understand, are nearly tongueless and incapable of making a noise. She was throwing them in a tub of water and letting them churn there for a week. They are by no means good swimmers, scalatoids; it was sheer desperation that was keeping them afloat. Hour after hour, day after day, they treaded in that water, silent, frantic, indomitable, constantly attempting to climb up on one another. I was in my daughter's room, one afternoon, looking for my razor, when I made the discovery of five of them in a washtub at the foot of her bed.

I hope never again in my life to see the like of what was in their eyes. It would be impossible to overestimate their fear of water and drowning. Scalatoids are vaguely globular creatures, full of surface and other tensions; and, forever after this, they seemed to me to be the embodiment of pure will.

(This, of course, was her way of burning up the excess fat.)

I put a stop to it immediately. Still, I must confess, I rather miss the things. There is no doubt about it: the struggle improved the flavor.

*　*　*

When we first moved to this area, it took me some time to realize that this is no ordinary place. Animals can be killed here but nothing dies naturally. It is a very special locus built on a confluence of singularities. The electric atmosphere plays subtle tricks of energy. On an otherwise bright day a bolt of lightning can *condense* itself out of the air. One can feel the static even in the soil itself, which has special properties. Part of the area may have been an island at one time, despite the largely sedimentary rock. There are signs, too, of a previous habitation (some fruit trees, for instance, not local to the area).

What is incredible is the extent the soil is layered and honeycombed with dormant animals. Having started from a slightly different angle, they have begun estivating through the millennia and running, somehow, parallel to death. They are tangled in places, clumped, like earthworms. In heavy storms they sometimes wash out of themselves. Fortunately, precious few of them are terribly large. The thought, though, of how they are layered here gravely bothers our occasional guests. My wife and I invariably hear them whisper to one another far into the night.

On first arrival, I paid little attention to the animals. I was so sick of academia, dazed and overrun that I did not want to expend any energy thinking. I ignored all implications and ate whatever was handy. I had worked too long and hard in a single line and it was as though I had wakened in the midst of a dream. Furthermore, much about these creatures was unfamiliar to me. Evidently there are evolutionary lines tangled here which did not proceed. I think there was a level at which I did not take them seriously; I expected them to fade, tooth and claw, at sunrise.

That was years ago. Now, I am fascinated once more. I have returned to my books and manuals and vowed never again to eat anything without a name.

Such persistent and single-minded endeavor is not without its dangers, however. One evening, not long ago, based on no more than intuition and a low mound, little-Frank and I discovered a large animal in the bog below the lake. We dug it out together. We were rather pleased with ourselves and each grabbed two of its legs in order to carry it back. *Little*-Frank, I persist in calling him, though at this point he is taller than I am. (In fact, the whole way home he complained that he had most of the weight.)

I was anxious to flip it over to see what was going on with its reproductive system; but by the time we got to the basement we were both too exhausted.

(It had three eyes and I knew it had to be a rather early specimen.)

Our basement gets very cold at night and I figured it would be safe there till morning. I couldn't begin to decide what to call it. This was the first one I'd ever caught and, in my ignorance of its strength, I looped a chain around its neck of scarcely more than half-inch links.

When I went upstairs, the wife was already in bed. The windows were shut and the lamps were lit. We augment our illumination with kerosene lamps. In fact, we keep one lit at the foot of the bed at all times. Our electricity is not reliable and I feel it is best to have a bit of light instantly available, being as what we are surrounded by out here. "Honey..." I said, but lost my train of thought.

I began wiping my feet together over the side of the bed. I couldn't get the thing out of my mind; it seemed to have scales; it definitely had claws; I was not altogether happy about it. The lamp on the nightstand had just been extinguished and there was a pale glow of red from the wick.

"It might not be a reptile," I said.

At three in the morning, I woke up. It sounded like there was something in the basement swacking around with a four-by-four. I got out of bed immediately. But my son was already in the room. He turned up the lamp till it smoked. The light was swinging, the whole cabin shuddering at each blow.

"Frank, it's loose!" he said.

"What?"

(I began fumbling around on the night table for my glasses.)

"It's *loose*, Frank!"

I slipped on boots, got my Luger out of the closet, grabbed the prong and the gig and went out the back way, tripping on the stairs. I ran around to have a look in through a basement window.

I have a workshop at one end. The creature had dragged through the tools for that, tangled himself in the cables for the arc welder and begun chewing on the vise. A piece of the chain was still attached to his neck. I got around to the closest window, broke out the pane, and, using the flashlight, began firing down through all the orbital foramina. The dog was barking hysterically. I reloaded the Luger five times and emptied the entire last clip down its throat.

Then I stopped and waited.

My daughter stood by, watching.

It took two full days for all motion to cease; the meat, when cut up, would not lie flat or lose its muscle tone. Even after being *cooked*, it seemed to positively creep on the plate. Never have I so underestimated a metabolism.

We got a total of seven pounds of thyroid tissue out of the thing, most of which, admittedly, may not have been active. The entire gland was goitrous and cystic and took a lot of chewing to get through.

"Always room in this world for surprises!" I said, somewhat lamely, when it was over, though nothing truly big is ever getting inside this house again in one piece.

The experience was terrifying, though the animal itself was, on the whole, rather straightforward. Not like everything we find here. Consider the one I discovered some years ago while planting the fig tree: He was about a yard long, completely legless, with a distinctly submarine-like shape and something of a beaver-like tail (the tail turned vertically, though). He had two close-set eyes and a single upturned nostril.

(The nostril, in fact, was the part of him I came upon first.)

The problem was that there was no way he could be placed on the ground that he would either balance or sit level. I kept playing with his cold body in the cold sand but he kept tilting or rolling over on me. Finally, I became frustrated and tossed him, end-over-end (he was as stiff as a log) into the lake. I thought no more about him. But, two years later, I found what was evidently the same guy, very much alive, placidly sculling around in the backwaters, keeping that single nostril above the surface of the water.

"Blah!" I said, suddenly very disappointed in myself.

(I felt then, as I do now, that his aquatic nature should have been obvious.)

The truth is, were that lake drained, that creature would not be the most interesting thing in it. My feeling is that the denizens of its depths must scarcely eat anymore. It contains a virtual *stew* of life-forms which have been coasting through that liquor for millennia. Such a collection is marvelously edifying, of course, though truthfully, what one has here, as in all evolution, is variety more than improvement.

(I have eaten plenty of the modern animals and they simply don't taste any better.)

Occasionally, I go fishing in the lake, most often with the wife or little-Frank, though at the last outing it was my daughter that wanted to accompany me. We keep a small steam launch at the end of the dock. My daughter insisted on riding in the very back of it and adorned herself, perfectly inappropriately, in a flowing dress and a straw hat with purple ribbons. (So that's it, I thought, she wants to wear her new hat.) It took her some time to arrange her body on the cushions in the stern. We went chugging out slowly, with my doing all the stoking of coal and adjusting of valves. I locked the tiller and busied myself screwing down grease cups, the vapor and smoke settling around us on the black water. There was a disquieting calm within the lake and in the huge trees that overhung it. Every time I looked back at her, I found my daughter watching me, those purple ribbons trailing behind.

(Some of her proclivities I worry about.)

We—or rather I—fished all day but caught nothing interesting: a dozen catfish, a few trout, and a small amphibian which resembled a hellbender. While chugging back, the pump to the condenser broke which put us another forty-five minutes behind. It was nearly sunset when we got home. It was then that I found we had only one fish in our tank. I was furious considering the total effort expended and demanded to know what had happened to the rest of them. Surprisingly enough, my daughter did not hesitate to say:

She had been poking their eyes out with her hat pin and releasing them into the water.

We walked to the cabin with a dreadful silence between us. I didn't know what to say. The worrisome thing about my daughter is that she will do anything she thinks of. This is a trait she gets from her mother, who, when she is in a bad mood, has been known to clean an animal alive. Our pathetic catch—one short and rather fat catfish—I carried in myself, holding it by the tail. I was disgusted and didn't even bother to kill or clean it. My wife has a tin-lined copper pot which holds eight gallons. When placed on the stove (which is where I put it) the pot appears huge and overlaps two burners. I filled the bottom of it with water and watched my fish swim in circles inside. I sliced some wedges of lemon (two of which it gobbled whole). Then it began to nibble at a third. Afterward, the fish seemed to notice some shadow of itself reflected in the bright tin and thereupon began to make what seemed to be threatening, territorial gestures toward it.

"Blah!" I said, slicing another lemon. "The fruit of our labors!"

The fish circled and returned to its illusory companion. I watched it more carefully. The movements began again. Perhaps they were not territorial at all; perhaps they were gestures of courtship.

"Who knows?" I said, lighting both of the burners.

The anger and fire in the eyes of animals is not unrelated to the motion of the body. If one holds them perfectly still, there is a vulnerability which appears in the pupils that one can look deeply into. We found this out largely by accident thanks to a method we sometimes use to marinade creatures while they are still alive. (We bind them with ropes to wooden boards and platters.) Even in the most vicious the look will be there. In the mammals it is very obvious; in others, it can be obscured by a surface glitter. I have come to think of the pupil as a two-way mirror, a dark portal both reflecting and opaque. I know not what the brain behind it makes of us, but always before I make ready the pots and sever the cord, I bow down at the point of focus and offer myself as if to a god.

The endless dying with so little visible birth contributes to the melancholy atmosphere in this place. We have cold and snow, heat and rain; but no winter or spring, no face to the seasons here. Far more than the times are out of joint; there seems to be some fundamental dislocation to life itself.

I find myself wondering on occasion, "Why isn't there any central *trunk* anymore? Why is everything out on a limb?" Sometimes in my despair, I will turn to the invertebrates, gaze at a cluster of eyes on stalks and ask: "Where did we go wrong?"

In our den I have started a museum of sorts of a taxidermic nature. I spend much time in the basement, too, rubbing arsenic into skins. In order that nothing go unappreciated, I have been working on a book with some recipes. My wife thinks this an egregious waste of time. However, it was thanks to this particular endeavor that I discovered the possibilities of the thip-lo.

"Gentlemen!" I used to tell my students. "Never underestimate the principles involved! Most of life has nothing to do with living!"

(Cooking is but chemistry, after all. Here is what I found.)

The thip-lo[3] is quite a local animal, dull grey, and reminiscent of a tadpole. It is limited to four ponds nearby which are scarcely larger than mud puddles. Thip-loes are naturally sluggish but when placed in fingerbowls of wine they begin to move faster and afterward become very active in the light. The alcohol doesn't seem to harm them; they swim in loops, it is true, but the motion itself is colorful in its way. They dress up a table, like parsley. As individuals, they are curious-looking, with a single median eye, lidless, in the pineal area, though there are also vestigial rudiments of other eyes, appearing like tiny warts in front. (Thus there is a sort of pseudo-face on their anterior aspect.) The mouth is very ventral so that, like skates and rays, they can't really see what they are eating. They are toothless but this is perhaps a degenerate state as they seem to have well-developed little gums. Though very limited in their habitat, they nevertheless reproduce surprisingly rapidly. (Indeed, they always seem to be interested in one another.)

As an experiment, I kept several in cold water and out of the light over the length of a summer. Under such conditions, they can grow to a hideous size. They are tougher then, somewhat stringy, a double handful: much more slimy, too, and rather difficult to catch.

Far more interesting, though, is a another change:

When small, I would not say thip-loes are *cute*, exactly, but there is a definite sadness to them. If ever there was an animal completely "at the mercy…" The change that comes with increased size is not alone of dimensions but of character: something *evil* seems to come out in them.

I consigned my bloated experiments to the furnace, dropping the heavy iron lid on their noiseless writhing in the flue. Thip-loes make mainly passive sounds in flames, a vicious bubbling and hiss. Nevertheless, the whole experience was disturbing to me. I felt very much like the alchemists of old at morning: haggard and sleepless.

There can be no catharsis in work doomed mostly to fail.

Fortunately, none of this affected my appetite for the smaller form. One can toss a dozen in a huge brandy snifter of an evening and let them loop for hours in the yellow wine. I hope it is not blasphemous to say so, but very God-like I feel with a bowl of thip-loes by the fire. Even a small snack gives much to chew upon. How quickly they exit the living state! They make a distinct pop when chewed, not

unlike caviar, and are best, I think, with a good thick cheese
dip which keeps them from flipping about so much.
Occasionally, I will find myself turning one so it can see
me—or what is *eating* it, as the case may be. No more than
a bubble, it seems, a rubbery pop.

But I suppose the least of the dead know the secrets of
death.

Sometimes, I think a good part of what I have is akin to
an archaeological interest. I imagine myself in Pompeii or
Crete and the first to find an ancient mosaic on a floor. A
sweep with my broom will reveal a ridge of horny scales or
skin, the curve of a tail, possibly an eye, which after being
uncovered will begin to look about.

"Gentlemen! (as I used to say) What you are truly
trapping in field-biology, is *perspective*, not consciousness!"

One must always separate the creatures from the soil.
They can't be reliably killed in situ. Indeed, it is often
difficult to know when they are dead. Many of the animals
have to be pried up with a crowbar and I cannot sufficiently
emphasize the importance of trying to estimate the full
extent of the perimeter and account for all appendages
before beginning to lift one out.

(The animals are often mud-colored themselves and it's
easy to be misled by a close-set pair of eyes.)

Altogether, our days are not unpleasant; life is not
fundamentally different in this place, only more concen-
trated. What is most interesting is that the hierarchy within
our lake doesn't work out as advertised. Of course it is
probably unfair to have all the animals in the same *pot*, so to
speak, at the same time. Still, it is sobering to see how
quickly one of your stupid old crossopterygians can chew
up a teleost.

The black water of the lake and the slick calm of its
surface belie how much one can learn within and around it.
Every day is a discovery and an experiment. I am no longer

certain that it is only in humans that the religious practices can become part of the life cycle. There seems to be a great *piety* in the shallows here among the diplocauli with their upturned eyes. The truth is quite a few of the early creatures look very worshipful to me.

It is children that are inherently irreverent.

I must confess that, lately, I have been thinking along that line. Babies may exhaust a woman but they keep her from being moody. And there is no doubt my wife has been cantankerous recently. Just last week, we were digging near the bog with a hoe and potato rake. Despite the cold we were doing rather well, working on our second wheelbarrow-full, when suddenly she said she was not going to clean all these things. (She *would* wait till I had found a vein of them.) I was down on my knees now, yanking them loose from each other and the dirt. Where their skins abutted they were wet and slick as salamanders. I lost patience and began yelling at her:

"It's not just *food* we're after! We're completing the fossil record!"

(I heard nothing in response. After a while, I stood up and turned.)

She had thrown down her hoe and stormed off.

It was anger that had made me speak thus. In truth I know the record cannot be completed.

"Gentlemen! (as I would say, of old) There is *nothing* in between! It is like an organ pipe! Only certain modes can be supported! An ascending tone is not music! And what you see in the animals is the equivalent of chords!"

The truth is, I don't miss any of it. It was all too cumbersome and slow. How much of evolution is given over to the correct spacing of eyes?

Nevertheless, I can still reel off the lectures in my mind:

"Gentlemen! The environment's role is akin to tuning a *circuit*! It is akin to adding acid to precipitate something out of solution! The animal must be made *uncomfortable* in nonexistence!"

* * *

Gentlemen! Gentlemen!

Blah.

My wife is disgusted with me.

Sometimes I think we have no right to eat anything; that the goal of a good man should be to become a good skeleton, to have one's silent bones swept, disarticulate, amongst the rocks and minerals. In the meantime, I persevere; I am convinced of the importance of it all. With my gloved hands, I rub in arsenic in order to preserve some trace of the skins. I feel that the pursuit of knowledge is not incompatible with appetite. I look deeply into the eyes of the creatures we are preparing to kill, pray constantly, and arrange around us the food we have eaten. I work, perhaps, in the spirit of the great Wallace who ate blue macaws for breakfast. I don't know who will appreciate all of this. The truth is visitors are horrified by our den and by the leftovers in our refrigerator. They reproach us, I know.

What they think, I cannot imagine.

Still, I keep up my spirits as best I can.

My book of recipes is a major consolation. "Leviticus, Too," I plan to call it. When demoralized, I think of it as a discreet series of challenges. About the other (the *paranoia*, I mean) I really should not complain.

I suppose I am not the first father to feel his family is in conspiracy against him.

In order to get away from them, I began digging a new cistern. Day after day I worked at it, finding enormous relief in the sheer physical activity. To my surprise, I found absolutely nothing in the way of creatures. Then, at a depth of maybe twelve feet, my shovel struck something soft.

What I had hit, I seemed to have hit near the tail. I began to uncover the animal quickly, then afterward more carefully and finally at the full length of my broom and shovel. I could not bring myself to look at what I was doing. With what became a sudden appreciation of a great fear, I scrambled out of the hole and did the rest of my looking *down* at it. I had never seen the likes of the thing. It was huge by our usual standards, buried deeper, too, perfectly stupefied with age. Fully exposed, it was almost too nauseous to contemplate; it rattled my faith in everything I have ever believed in. There seemed to be flippers; there seemed to be claws; the five eyes were disturbingly arranged.

The creature looked frankly incomplete.

(If it were organized at all, it was in ways I never dreamed possible.)

I dug into the side of the cistern and fixed boards in a steep ramp to drag it out onto a tarpaulin with a block and tackle. It was nearly sunset and I was hesitant to leave it uncovered. I had my Luger, of course, but it does absolutely no good here to shoot anything until it moves. There was hardly any wind but the air was getting cold. It was supposed to snow during the night, so I hung the tarp on a rope between two trees.

Then I looked down again:

The eyes, which were not closed, were fixed forward, blankly. There was no obvious pupil to them. They resembled balls of granite.

The earth itself might have been staring up at me.

I returned to the house very slowly, lost in thought. It was true my academic era was over; still, in my heart I knew I was making daily what were great discoveries. I could not shake an abiding suspicion that I had been eating for years what I should have published. I saw, too, that what I had taken previously to be an occasional ugliness in animals was a complete illusion; I had vastly underestimated the power of symmetry.

"Gentlemen," I said (of a sudden, to an imaginary classroom in my mind), "we are not bowing *low* enough! We have prayed overlong to a two-handed God!"

I slept fitfully, if at all. Nevertheless, by morning I thought I knew the answer. True, this creature was odd to begin with, but what it is is *dead*; what it is is *dead* and partially decomposed. At such a level, the character of the soil may be somewhat different.

(Still, I reasoned, the meat itself might be good.)

I went outside. The air was bitterly cold and indeed it had snowed in the night. In my musings, I had almost passed the trees when I noticed that the tarpaulin I had hung up yesterday evening was missing. I looked around now and became much more hesitant. Then I went forward to the pit, crunching in the snow.

No, I thought.

The tarpaulin was in disarray at the bottom.

The animal was *not* dead. Evidently, it was a female, too, possibly of some vaguely mammalian inclinations. She had done her very best with the tarpaulin and her awkward flippers and claws to protect her babies from the cold. I could see them suckling in long rows beneath her, their thin skin almost translucent in the grey dawn. The blue ice had caught alike in the folds and ridges of canvas and their lidless and vulnerable eyes.

The snow of centuries would fall upon them now.

I looked down for some time. Then I returned to my bedroom. I brought out a blanket and took it to the pit, and, with a long stick, arranged it so that it wrapped and sheltered all of them. I cannot know whether the creature herself saw or understood me but she made no effort to move.

I walked back silently, very deep in meditation.

"This can destroy us," I thought.

In front of the cabin, my daughter was working on a huge form in the snow. "Hoo!" she said, when she saw me. She is a little too old to be making snow creatures. Moreover, her sense of proportion is flawed. There are some that would say it's because my daughter herself is fat. That is no matter; it will not be long now; she is some two years older than our son.

As I walked, I thought of the creatures sleeping beneath my feet, and how these were being shown unto us and how pleased we were with them. A more bountiful cornucopia could not exist. I cannot hope to understand what brought our little family to the midst of such plenty. It is more than I can do just to name these animals.

My wife was by herself in the house. It seems the two of us, alone, were to share a late breakfast. As she moved about the kitchen, I watched her smiling eyes, slightly yellow in the light. Evidently I am forgiven. She is in an amorous mood. We must have some more children soon. She had sautéed a platygast and stuffed it with raisins and slices of apple. I poured the syrup over the thin and purple-looking skin and, like a wave, an unexpected happiness came over me. Verily I say unto you, I have never been more content. I made a joyful noise and bowed my head in prayer:

"Bless this food, oh Lord. Bless all food, living or dead. Bless our children and the metamorphic world in which they live. Forget us not in our strange homes and forgive us our curious prayers, for in our souls we know the one point behind the eyes is central to all. Allow some considered share of thine infinite blessings to fall gently upon this house. This we ask in thy name, oh Lord, and in the name of whatever love or wisdom beats within the vastness of thy three-chambered heart."

"Amen," I added, picking up my fork.

---

[1]"Bone" *is* the correct word here (amazingly enough) not cartilage. Intramembranous ossification begins almost immediately in *Stelacens*—which, despite some superficial resemblances, are definitely *not* Elasmobranchii.

[2]Something of a common or popular name. (The teeth, though extremely tiny, are step-like.)

[3]Popular name. Sold in baitshops locally. Difficult to classify but almost assuredly amphibian.

PYTHON

My night is over, my work is done, and in the hours of waiting I hang heavily from my liana and allow the sun to ease into the sky. In a long and silent lull, I rest, subdue my breathing, and permit the fading moon to make more noise than I. There is a tunnel of grey, a time without interval, then a burning of fog and a spreading of insects and light. There is a pause as the moment arrives and I open my brain and organize the first thought of the day.

My first thought is always the same thought and forever the same thought and identical in every way. In the egg itself I thought it. It is no-thought; it is nothing; it is less than nothing: against the forces of day, I hold a perfect vacuum exactly centered in my mind. This is my inheritance and the province of reptiles alone. (Mammals who try it are crushed by the pressure.) No-thought has no shape or form, no weight or sound; it has only a color, the very *essence* of night, which the darkness itself obscures. Every morning, I hold this color very gently in my mind:

It is yellow, like the sun.

Night comes, then day, then another day and night. My mate is gone now and there is a wobbling duck in my cage. I watch him move, watch him watch and wait. Curious how the great momentums of life pass him by; sometimes a chicken, sometimes a duck, but always a bird, or of the birds, the great fidgeters of the world in my cage. Off my liana now I slide, and rest what is left of my chin against my boulder. Very steadily, I watch this duck. I can tell by the rims of his eyes how fully he appreciates the nature of the relationship between us. If I could say one thing to him, to this nervous duck (a good fowl) I would say what I wished to say in days of old to my husband when we were not speaking:

"You take yourself too seriously."

Patience. There is time. Time is what there always is.

Let us pause to digest the above.

In the last of the old lives, in the tall old house by the bay, there were long wooden tables in a greenhouse and on them aquariums of glass and iron. I had a son then, of a lazy demeanor (the tanks and fish were his) and a husband who called himself a politician.

How long ago this was, I cannot know. Perhaps it is pointless to say. After all, what characterization of time can there be in a series of numbers? I prefer to remember the period as I knew it then: it was the era of radio and fluorescent light.

Our home in those years had a courtyard which enclosed a pool and part of a greenhouse. My son took over this greenhouse in his teens and immediately disappeared inside it. Very odd, in fact, how in a *glass* house he could become so invisible. One could open the door and see nothing at all: a maze of bubbling aquariums, the cool and moldy brick floors, the huge fans and a few tall plants that gave shuddering evidence of a breeze through it at all times. My son had stacked and arranged the tanks so there were no clear lines of sight. Amid this labyrinth he would sit for hours with a single finger on a tank. There were times I thought he could *see* things in the water, things invisible to me. I would stand behind a stack of aquariums and watch him unobserved, think of his face reflected in the eyes of a thousand guppies, of the moving images of him there unimaginably wet and fragile.

He noticed me once and said:

"I wonder whether they are thinking a constellation of small thoughts or pieces of a large one."

"Thoughts!" (I thought). So very strange how variably the mind works. Too *active*, this word, thought.

What I felt I was seeing was memory.

It is day again. Our zoo is open. The humans have begun to arrive. Curious, isn't it, how they sort themselves by type? Here are two women in particular, very elegant and slim, whose hands have come down to a matter of pure articulation. I know well the cool feel of such fingers and that hair and all its strategies of endearment. Very glad, I am, that I no longer have to carry such a banner before the world. Nevertheless, I wish you would watch them watch me. For every ten who marvel at how long I am, there will be two who wonder what I am thinking. Scarcely one in a hundred will wonder what I am wondering.

But wondering, indeed, is the correct word.

I am *wondering*, my fine young females, how you would have liked my son.

Swimming alone in the pool, playing tennis against a wall, never fully awake till noon, the silent child, he looked good in clothes. Much room we had in that house together. My son had sandy hair, but strange to say, dark whiskers like a dust of charcoal in his pale skin. I never remember any childhood for him; no toys or teddy bears. From the earliest age he slept alone and concerned himself with the fit of silk ties and coats.

Sometimes, at night, in the summers, I would wander onto the upstairs porch, barefooted and restless in a green kimono, and sit on the ledge and smoke my cigarettes in the warm, moist wind from the bay. I would dangle my bare and human and impeccable legs over the railing and, far below, the concrete terrace for the pool. I would watch the windows of the greenhouse and imagine my son inside: the huge plates of sepulchral light, the long streaks of condensation, the awnings of striped canvas, the occasional loom of a misplaced shadow. I suppose that a morgue could not have looked more sinister. I would find myself wondering sometimes, what was he doing? Separating minnows? Watching the fanning of fins? Nurturing the frantic demons of his pumps? In the nights, in the heat, in the damp, rotting smell of the sea.

Long ago.

The women are gone now. My audience has disappeared. (*Malaca of old, I wish you could watch them watch me.*) Thus it will be all day long. I have not forgotten so much of my former life as to be unaware of when I am on display. My mate, the smaller, the slower of mind (the dolt as I call him) has decided to intrude upon my memories and warmth. He seems happier when we are layered together. But this is not necessarily a love knot we are tied into. To be sure, it took me some time to grow accustomed to the caresses of a snake. I remembered too well the human touch, the words like a mantra when the neck is being massaged, the hair being stroked or rearranged, the soft manipulative voice:

"Do you know how beautiful you are?"

(So many men in the old days came down to asking me that, that in truth I began to suspect the answer.)

In those days, in those summers, in the age of radio and fluorescent light, one could begin to undress by the Zenith in the upstairs hall, remove one's blouse near the Atwater Kent, then tiptoe, barefooted, into the cool silence of the garage, enter the Packard and with knees together slide off one's panties near the luminous dial of the Philco.

There were nights when only the cat knew my whereabouts.

Perfectly naked in the leathery bulk of the automobile, sitting behind the long hood, sinking my teeth into the steering wheel, I would spread my legs apart, place my hands against my thighs, and feel the moist air breaking with a sudden and frustrating lightness into me.

Indeed, there is nothing I miss about being human the way I miss my Packard.

I was not a large woman then, or Amazonian; I was delicate but fearless and with a highly *functional* anatomy. As humans will, I had gathered around me friends of a similar shape and inclination. What this group was initially, I don't remember; in fact, can't imagine. (Can't *imagine,* mind you, the wherefore of my own past). I only know what it became; we were not exactly a social gathering; we had gone beyond all social considerations.

We could have become a coven, perhaps, had we worshipped anything but ourselves.

We were guided in our endeavors by a woman named Malaca. She, it was, who posed the tasks, asked the questions, demanded, criticized and punished. Very cool, she stood, beneath the dark mirrors. Amid the crystal chandeliers, polished silverware, decanters and painted china, the white creams and spices from the darkest tropics (and the flakes of a salt made from sea water), we met; and in this simple laboratory, I discovered complex things:

I discovered that a silver spoon stirring gently in a silver bowl makes the sound of tin.

This delectable Malaca was a creature of rules and discipline. Her strengths were more than physical and the only clue to any *deficiency* of mind was that she knew what she thought about everything. She once gave us the task of making a soup with the essence of a pearl, the essence of a *pearl,* she said, which had nothing to do with whiteness or opacity.

(The essence of a pearl was *triumph* as the essence of a diamond was fire.)

Her long fingers at my throat, her silver-streaked hair obscuring one eye, she would feed me till I nearly choked in swallowing. "That is better, isn't it?" she might say, "almost transparent, but with a darker flavor."

Who was this soup *for*, though? Ourselves or our virginal daughters? Of course, I had no daughter but a son who had grown beautiful. Thus we pondered, compared and reminisced. Thus we became sultry and hard to please. During these evenings we were allowed to wear one thing only. I wore, always, a pair of dark stockings folded onto my thighs: slim, pale, firm and aromatic as candle wax. I felt suffused with the glow of the wine, the weight of the mirrors and shadowy chandeliers. I would look upward, roll my neck, close my eyes then open them. The high, dark, ceiling looked wet above; and in the dangling prisms the points of light seemed like the eyes of a thousand guppies looking down at us.

The youngest member of our group we had come to call The Child. Though fully twenty-six years old, there was that juvenile quality in her blonde hair and face. She could maintain that attitude and innocence through a dozen orgasms. Eminently spoiled, I suspect we made as many efforts as her husband did to please her. At times, affectionate, cuddly, irritable or sleepy, we took turns kissing her pouting lips. Once, two of us were on her; but Malaca had become dominant and in the final throes of her passion, nearly bit her ear off in the process of whispering into it.

"Grow *old* little bitch, grow old."

This, with no real spite or viscousness; it was more like adding salt to something, not necessarily a wound.

(She did, too, I might add, though not that night.)

The child was upset at this. But Malaca was unrepentant: "I remind you, we have some interest in truth, none in justice."

"You were always heartless."

"I was worse than that. I was a ballerina."

(Beneath the silver chafing dish, the alcohol flame made the sound of an open mouth; and within the froth of blue, the swirling sparks gave a drifting grit of light.)

I remember a dissatisfaction during this whole time, but not a sexual frustration. My lover in that era was of an ancient and undemocratic style. The Praetor I called him; and, indeed, I could easily imagine him in a Roman toga.

Tangled in his arms, doubling back to sink my teeth into his ribs, moving forward again to kiss his mouth, his grey temporal hair, his athlete's body, I would clamp my hands in the coarse hair of his chest and poise my lips at the base of his throat.

"We could chew through right here, my dear, gnaw off this head and you would be a young man again."

The Praetor's body smelled of powder. He would put his hand well inside me to lift me onto the bed. Somehow we would become engaged and he would try to drive me over the edge. I knew that to fall off would be to lose and would use the full strength of my abdomen to fight him, find myself drowning in a faint of exhaustion, our perfectly enameled teeth locking in a duel, scraping slightly as in the bind and envelopment of sabers. There were times I had to restrain myself from biting into his lower jaw, attempting to shatter and fracture it like rock candy. I remember well the feel of our teeth together, this curious, this harder-than-bone thing, this *brittle* aspect to our passion.

He would parry the attack and want another kiss.

"Well very well. But remember, dear, most animals kill with their mouths."

I had infinite license with the Praetor, I'm afraid, but with my collaborators one night, I violated the rules: I wore lipstick to one of our meetings.

On arrival I felt more conspicuous than I had expected. Malaca ignored me at first, but as the evening wore on began to move toward me, to stalk and corner me like a cat. She backed me up until I found myself sitting nude on the tablecloth. Then she wet one finger in my glass of wine, placed it on the rim, and began to circle the bell. She derived from it a pure tone of such roaring volume as nearly filled the room.

Then she stopped the vibration.

"No," she said, dipping into the wine again, beginning to wipe the lipstick from my mouth. I hung my head, looking at her alabaster groin, my desire for her as thick as lanolin. (True decadence is in no way separable from intelligence; the rest is but spasm and impulse.) I felt my smearing lips, saw her greying pubic hair, and, on the tablecloth, a knife with white crabmeat on the blade.

I brought my knees closer together as though chastised.

"Never," she said. "No make-up. No paint. That is for elsewhere. I want to see the clear dew of sweatiness along your forehead and throat."

Malaca's nails were clear, trimmed to perfection, but her fingers appeared bloody when she had finished with me. Her one thing to wear was a man's aviator's watch of military issue. It fit loosely on her wrist, like a bracelet. "It is pointless to attack me, my dear. I cannot be destroyed. Don't you see what I am?" She came closer. I shrugged, tossed my hair over my shoulder and began to quiver inside. She raised my chin and slapped me sharply: "I am the triumph of form over substance and of personality over intellect."

I heard the steady ticking of her watch and saw in her soft and perfect breasts, the pink knots of her nipples.

"Anyway, my dear, the red lips are for men. If you want a woman, you must color them otherwise." She began to knead the muscles of my neck then leaned forward and licked the place she had slapped. She turned to the sideboard behind her and poured from a decanter of crème de menthe. "One glass will do for two. Come here." She brought her mouth close to mine and pulled me into her. "Like this."

For a moment I tried to fight her sidelong tongue.

"And what is this?" she said, knocking my left hand away from her groin. "*In*stinct?"

Then she released me:

"I want to borrow your son. Tomorrow afternoon. Send him to my house on an errand."

I swallowed heavily but did not answer.

"Like this again," she said.
This time, she left my hand alone.

In truth, it was not so long after my rebirth that I saw instinct for what it was: a form of communication between the living and the dead. There was a hollowness in my life which I remember, even now, from my great thickness and weight. I could not seem to get *at* that woman. I needed a form of reassurance that was not forthcoming. The Praetor was of no help whatsoever. The ultimate insult and slap to the "other" woman—which, at other times, I *was* of course —is to know that even in the most purely physical encounters, your partner desires his own wife more. The only weakness that I knew of in this man was a serious fear of heights. On the ground, however, the Praetor was more than invincible. Still, it would have been neither malicious or necessary to introduce him to Malaca.
He was her husband.

The following afternoon, I arranged things as Malaca had asked. Not surprisingly, my self-centered son was annoyed at a change in his plans. I had to force him to dry his hands and go to the aid of this woman. He paused on the way out of the greenhouse and took the time to feed an oscar, slowly dropping the gritty food on the surface of the water. I saw a certain brightness in the fish's eyes, though its body looked retarded to me. I found myself watching the fish, my son, then the fish again, its pectoral fins askew. There was a moment I could have sworn there was a plot between them.
I felt very strongly that Malaca was going to be disappointed in my son. I waited for him all afternoon but it was full evening before I saw him again. When I did, there was no word said, not the slightest change in his mood or behavior. After dark, the lights went on as usual in the greenhouse, the shadows circled as before. In the days that followed, I could not say that one thing was new or

different about him. Still, I saw somewhat less of him than usual, though his tanks never went untended, the fish never went unfed. The only change that I saw came elsewhere and in my group of friends and collaborators:

I saw their eyes sparkle when I entered the room.

I found myself beginning to watch my son more carefully. When he wore his white shorts, I would stare at the blonde hair on his legs and wonder what order of things I did not know about him. At twilight, standing at my bedroom window, I would follow the headlights of the Packard as they turned in and swept the lawn. Once, on his way out the front door, tennis racquet in hand, he tossed the cat overhead and behind him into the chandelier.

But no one in my group ever said anything to me about him.

For my part, I began entering the greenhouse more often, trolling amid the silent fish for information, not about my son, I think, but about my group of collaborators. I began to feel there was something about them I had overlooked. I watched the colorful fish waltz and pirouette, watched the neon splotches of yellow and red, the jars of water with layered gravel; the water with guppies, or tetras, or angel fish—the water with nothing but light dissolved inside. What answers could be within these tanks? What questions? The colors themselves had begun to look artificial to me. I realized I had never been more sure my son was *seeing* something amid the bubbles. (I was certain, too, that the something he was seeing was moving in different directions than the fish.)

I began to feel isolated and restless. In reaction, I began walking barefoot, almost stalking, in the upstairs hall. We had remodeled and were more than up-to-date; we had our thick carpeting wall-to-wall, our long tubes of indirect light, our stone statues and ikebana, our blue and shadowless illumination and our mirrors where one's lipstick would appear the color of lead.

My question was: through my son were my friends possessing me or themselves? Had he become a sort of mirror for them, an intersection for fluid and groin? How strange it is that in the most beautiful women one can see exactly where an external genitalia should fit. I became the victim of an undirected jealousy and was surprised to discover the extent to which jealously needs no object but can exist as a thing apart, like a whirlwind.

The truth is, I had begun to mistrust this decadence. There were times, between the locked doors and shuttered windows, while tying a silver stocking around a golden ankle, I had what amounted to a *fear* that no one was watching. It seemed I had misunderstood both the nature and extent of our abandonment; there were no depths to depravity, no darkness even; it was a surface phenomenon, perhaps as truly colorless as the wings of butterflies. What could we possibly think we were stealing here?

Time itself was easing us off the planet.

I felt cheated by the situation and by my son and his maddening adolescence. The very freshness of his face began to annoy me. I could not penetrate his eyes, could form no gauge to his character; too perfectly balanced, he seemed, though the balance was not between good and evil. I would watch him re-puttying an aquarium or dabbing paint with a small brush on a strip of angle iron and find myself at a loss to decide whether he was serene or silly. Two tiny girls rescued a starfish from a tide pool and brought it to him in a glass jar. He seemed grateful at the time, but I later found he had sliced it up and fed it to his turtles.

"You don't like stars?" I asked.

(We were on the tennis court at the time. He dropped a ball, caught it, then dropped it again.)

"They make too much noise," he said.

Always somnolent, always unconcerned, always the bastard, I would say (though I knew better). I had begun to ignore these open-ended statements of his that passed for wisdom. Quite honestly, I never thought he was truly intelligent, merely confused, like Socrates.

Well.

Another duck this week. Simple beasts, these ducks, with their metallic quacking; simple birds, more correctly, but of a lazy concept, their bodies retaining, still, the form of the egg. Let him waddle and keep himself warm; let him watch and wait. How can one doubt the wisdom of the carnivores when the best-tasting animals are kept simmering at all times?

I am within sight in this cage of other creatures that are purported to be my cousins; there is a family of Gila monsters in an enclosure nearby. The fat old female has a skin of warty excrescences and part of a front foot missing. I'm not as attuned to these animals as I should be. In fact, I only clearly understood one message between them; it came from the male one afternoon, pitched in a low and guttural vein and translates (very literally, I mean):

"Do you know how beautiful you are?"

The day wanes; from the low height of my liana I allow the cool blood to course through my simmering brain. There was a time when I was happier in this configuration, when every move, every motion, was like the first stretch in the mornings of old, a watching of sunlight through lace, and nothing to do but brunch. The novelty has passed; I am bored now; there seems to be no place in this cage for ulterior motives. Even the dolt serves only to *remind* me of someone from my previous life (I have confessed as much to him in the past) but to what purpose I cannot know, since every day he mostly ignores me.

One might well ask, though, where did the old life go? What was the *nature* of the transition? To remember is not so difficult. What is difficult is to be satisfied with the answer.

The truth is my present state had nothing to do with death;
it began when a great sleepiness entered my life. I was not
dead on the way to the cemetery. I was not even in the
casket. I was smoking a cigarette in the family car.

(Indeed, it was not *my* funeral.)

The road to the cemetery was newly paved and felt
as smooth as marble under the tires. I was oblivious to
many things, but I soon noticed that the feel of the heavy
limousine was not unlike my Packard. In the great solem-
nity, I began to wonder, would the desire somehow come to
remove my clothes? This enormous automobile seemed far
more masculine to me than my fat husband who preceded
us now in his fat casket—and who, perhaps, was not
masculine at *all* at this point.

The bright fields were lined with dark cars and a black
van passed us for the network transmission. The marines in
their white gloves waved us through the intersections. The
skin of my knees made a color like cream through my flexed
stockings, and I fiddled with a cigarette case made of
golden chains. Ahead of us, through the small windows at
the rear of the hearse, I found myself looking at the spray of
flowers on my husband's casket. I began to wonder
whether I could approach the *edge* of lust and be carried
over by the momentum. Beneath the thin silk of my dress,
the flesh of my buttocks began to feel as tight as a plum. I
felt like some schoolgirl who is learning the trick of crying
or a sneeze. The cortege slowed so that the casket was no
more than twenty feet ahead, then no more than twelve, no
more than six. Suddenly, I smiled spontaneously. How close
was I getting to the *trick* of desire?

In the pervasive silence, I watched the bells of the lilies in
the turns.

* * *

The lights are on. (I keep forgetting there are lights in this
jungle.)

Then the lights are off again.

The days pass so slowly now. If I had eyelids, I might close them eternally. I have grown testy with boredom. I have a hangover of sorts. I am in the mood to begin kicking off silk sheets. I long to stand fully erect then topple and slam my body against the earth, like a felled tree. There is a sign above me giving my dimensions. I am nineteen feet and one hundred and eighty-seven pounds of life...Life, Life! LI—FE! (I make myself nauseated at times.) Seduce me, dolt. It's the only way I have ever liked to wake up. Besides, there can't possibly be enough little *snakes* in the world.

After all, what effect does a mate have on me...truly?

Perhaps no greater effect than my androgynous son of old had on his lovers. I came to imagine them staggering into door frames and dragging their hands along walls. I wonder, though, in the moment of truth. (The moment of truth is a moment of lies.) Did they think a constellation of small thoughts or pieces of a large one?

I am awake. Or so it seems. Strange. Sometimes, even without sleeping, I find myself awakening. There seems to be a dove in our cage. I wonder why, or how? It can't be feeding time. My dolt seems to have noticed it as well. I watch as he moves, moves again, then follows, follows. What can I say, little dove? This is my *lover* that glares at you. When I was captured, a total of forty-six eggs were crushed in the swamp. What a waste! But something there is that likes reproduction better than life.

The dolt has frightened our dove. Patience, my love; it is the one reptilian trait you lack. The truth is, I have begun to take an interest in this bird myself. It is possible that the hunger I feel is for no more than food.

I shall recruit myself and move out like an army.

Well.

Look at what has happened. Surely we could never have planned such a trick. Get your mouth off *my* dove, dolt; I doubt we can tear it in two. This is quite a chance you are taking; I am larger, remember, a great deal larger. What if I have grown weary of loving you?

No answer, now, from the dolt, no comprehension, either, evidently. (His eyes are like two asterisks on a field of gold.) Come closer, then, my love. Would you like a long French kiss? Allow me to unhinge my jaws. What blind alleys are you prepared to go howling down, if only you could howl. Curious creature that you are, tell me what you see. Do you see red? Do you see green? Do you see all those colors that a *fish* can be?

Interesting, this feeling, this slow and thorough feeling, uncomfortable, but not without its value as both entertainment and sensation. Do not move, my pigeon, my love; and do not change your mind; your mind is no longer yours to change. Exhale gently and wind down this life; I shall save you the trouble of filling your lungs again. Come morning, our friends the humans will be back. Wait till they see what I have done. I shall have you nearly swallowed by then. An unaccustomed stiffness will pervade my being. Through my teeth, I shall hear their heels on the boards. There is supposed to be an *enmity*, you know, between our seed and theirs, between their heels and our heads. But I'm sure all of that is a vast oversimplification. Haven't you noticed, dear, we come very close to having heels ourselves. Strange, isn't it? I'm certain in my previous life I did not know that snakes could have even the rudiments of legs.

Your heavy heart beats so slowly inside my ribs. Is it the power of life or of death that grips you now? Allow me to whisper the answer with light, as gentle as a yellow wind sifting through trees, as endless as time and the source of this blackness. Perhaps I have not been honest with you; the truth is I've known for some years who you remind me of. Can you guess? I would think from such a vantage point you should be able to *see*. Think carefully, look very hard now, moving elegantly in the near distance...

You remind me of Malaca, my dear. She is, you know, that *thing* in the aquarium, besides the fish and plants, which is always there in the water. Now up on one foot, now on a single toe, dancing, whirling, the ballerina.

(It makes one almost sleepy to think about it.)

I am positive that in my previous life I did not know that snakes could have even the rudiments of legs. But every day I see them now, like little *spurs* in the region of my pelvis. They *move* for me at my desire. I wonder what they mean, exactly.

GENESIS
(The G.I. Bleed)

Y ou haven't missed much; the blood itself (beginning), the flashing lights, the sound: the drone, the hesitation, the burps, the counterpoint, and other electronic silliness that passes for a siren nowadays. The ambulance has just arrived at the dock. In a moment, the stretcher will be bumping through the doors. We are aware of what we are about to receive, though there may be some doubt as to whether or not we are truly grateful. Fortunately, we are not busy. There is not even one other patient in all of the green-tiled rooms of our emergency department. We have twelve beds, every one of them empty. This is a rare event, extraordinary even. Such profound quietness in an emergency room late at night is odd, spooky and any reference to it essentially blasphemous. (E.R. personnel are as reverent as gamblers.)

The stretcher enters now with two EMTs, male and female, pushing it. The stretcher itself is tubular, spindly, with ridiculously small wheels. The tallest of the EMTs is already talking: "Mr. R... (I didn't catch his first name) Collan, forty-three year old male, vomiting blood since nine o'clock this evening. Pressure 78 over palp. Pulse 138. Respirations thirty-five. History of pancreatitis, history of chronic E-T-O-H abuse. No diabetes. No hypertension.

(The other EMT is looking along the side of the stretcher.) I listen, but do not move. This is my third eight-hour shift in a row and I had not slept before the first one. I am exhausted and worn out. I am quite unreasonably tired. My brain feels bloody with fatigue. Were it not for this patient's arrival, I could be heading for bed. It could take hours now, depending on the exact scenario, to deal with him. What I should do is kill this patient.

I find myself watching the tight blue pants of the female EMT, the black plastic handles of the scissors in her back pocket, her cellular phone, the firm curve of her buttocks. I have already seen the patient's face, though. His face is classic. I don't mean the pallor, sweating, or diaphoresis, but the overall aspect. The faces are strangely interchangeable in these chronic alcoholics who have at last come down to their G.I. bleed; what we see in them is the *spirit* of exsanguination. The patient is anxious and embarrassed, like a dog that has just urinated on the rug or a man that can't stop farting in public. He is breathing rapidly, shallowly, carefully, trying not to jiggle his body. For once, he is paying some attention to his life.

There is a commotion now, a problem with the stretcher to which he is being transferred.

—Damn!

(We all hate these stretchers.)

—Mr. Collan! Let loose of the rail! Mr.Collan! Let loose of the *rail*!

—Grab him!

(Mr. Collan is jittering all over, flapping, like a large bird. He is saying something like, Ehhh, ehhh, ehhhhh, fu-ha fu-ha. Son of a *bitch*!)

—Mr. Collan!

At the sound of his name, Mr. Collan convulses twice. Suddenly, there is a black stream oozing from his mouth. Three nurses, wearing pale rubber gloves, are pulling at sheets, folding and manipulating him. Mr. Collan has grabbed the rail again. There is something stuck and dangling now in the crushed stubble of his beard. A monkey could not have grabbed the rail of this stretcher tighter. (A monkey!) In the pause, I see a bowel movement, black as tar, spewing out of his rectum. Then Mr. Collan's flabby buttocks are in the air. He vomits, then vomits again, though *wretches* is probably the better term, the vomitus twisting out of his body.

The EMTs are still talking. The pulse is 138. The bed at the scene was covered with black blood and coffee grounds. He is not known to have varices. They couldn't get a line.

(Only the fact that he may not have varices is good news.)

I move over and sit on an adjacent stretcher. This Mr. Collan is rather interesting. He is bald-headed with a blue snake tattooed to his forehead; there is an earring in his left earlobe. His face is pierced in three places. How old, did they say he was? Forty-three? A bit old for this particular appearance, a bit young for such a bleed. G.I. bleeds are rather common things. In fact, a bleed in and of itself is nothing; we may see two a night; it is the *extent* of a bleed that is of importance. A truly major bleed is somewhat rare, surprisingly so, actually. (Palp, though, they said; 78 over *palp*) which means there is no bottom number to the blood pressure. The patient is suspended over a void.

This is going to be a major G.I. bleed.

At the moment, everyone is touching the patient but me. The nurses are slapping up and down his arms, searching with large-bore Angiocaths, the needles and catheters which will be used for the infusion of IV fluids and blood. The nurses are working as fast as is humanly possible. They are collectively impatient. *They,* I say. I myself am merely sitting on a stretcher. A vulture has less patience than I. The truth is, there is something extra going on with me tonight. As I've said, I am quite *unreasonably* tired; I am in a speculative and dangerous mood. I have been in this mood before, and strange and puzzling, not altogether understandable, things have evolved from it. Visions, I think, visions.

To the clerk, who has come in and is standing for no good reason—curiosity perhaps—beside me, I say call G.I. and let them know what we have. G.I. (gastroenterology, G.I. we abbreviate it for some reason) will have to come in and scope the patient to find the exact source of the bleeding. Not just tonight, but immediately, I say, or think I say. I'll talk to them if they like, I say. (Or think I say.) Something like that. Something like that is what I say.

The clerk leaves and I use the opportunity to look at the blood in the basin. In truth, it is important to look at the blood. Despite my dangerous mood, I am pondering; and my pondering adds an extra ingredient to the mix. I feel something like an Indian scout of old, paying attention to the animal tracks, to the broken grass and twigs, to the leaves and puddles on the ground. The great majority of the blood is dark and watery. There is something that looks like tar and black jelly. There are some large clots. All of this is of no particular interest. There is something else, though, something that looks *red* in a crescent near the perimeter of the bowl. In certain oriental soups you find a similar something. This red something is to be paid attention to.

I hear a prolonged low hissing noise and soon thereafter a quick beep. The beep is from the automatic cuff of the blood-pressure monitor. 79/22 it says. (Pronounced 79 over 22.) The machine thinks there is a bottom number now to the blood pressure. Not *much* of a bottom number, mind you; the void has a floor of glass.

(Then too, it is the machine that is thinking.)

The nurses are finding nothing in his arms. Finally, the head nurse looks up at me. She is a blonde, currently wearing her hair in a loose ponytail held together by a pink bow. Her husband is an orthopedist with a huge practice in the suburbs. When this blonde is not torturing males with large-bore catheters she tools around in a convertible BMW with the top down.

—Guess what? she says.

I guess, reply, in fact:
—Wonderful.
This reply (*my* reply) the nurse interprets, of course, as sarcasm. I am still sitting on the stretcher. I am somewhat intimidated by her prolonged stare. Her eyes are as green as emeralds, perhaps as unlucky. I cannot believe any amount of schooling can get such a woman to listen to me. Her interpretation normally would be correct. Normally, I say. But I am not quite normal tonight. What I mean tonight is different, more literal. What I mean tonight is great.
(What I mean is perfect.)
—You want a syringe?
I shake my head, no.
In passing the head of the stretcher, I cannot resist touching the blue snake that is tattooed on the patient's forehead. (It is damp, cold with sweat: diaphoretic, as is the patient.) The patient, of course, is in shock; a tough guy, no doubt, in other circumstances; it's a good thing the women are handling him. Suddenly, I find that I have fallen asleep standing beside the stretcher. Then I am awake, or seem to be.
I put on a pair of gloves and sweep Mr. Collan's damp testicles aside.
What the head nurse has told me with the words "Guess what?" is that this patient is a drug addict. We are not going to be able to get blood from his peripheral veins. We are going to have to go elsewhere, where he normally doesn't think or dream of going. We are going to his groin now where, despite the low pressure, I can already feel the femoral artery. The artery is not bounding, but then again, not so thready either. I feel it very distinctly. I then go slightly medially to where I feel absolutely nothing at all. The patient's skin is raw-looking, pale and hairy. This is where the femoral *vein* is...or is supposed to be. (*Is*, in this case; a thin jet-like fountain begins spattering into the Vacutainers.) I hand the glass tubes, like test tubes, with rubber stoppers, to the head nurse. She rocks them back and forth to keep them from clotting. I find myself watching a

silver bracelet on her left wrist, her wedding rings under the rubber glove.

I wait, looking down at the patient, holding pressure on his femoral vein.

God knows how much he has lost.

—I'm going to need a triple-lumen, I say.

Actually, I'm going to need a number of other things, too, all of which will take a minute or so to find and set up. In the meantime, I hold pressure on Mr. Collan's vein, trying not to make it too obvious that I am leaning against him, propping my exhausted body up with my fingers. I have discovered through the years that I very much like holding pressure on large blood vessels; it is something to do, something essential, something no one is going to make you *stop* doing. But those are not the only reasons, or even the main one:

It's like being in the eye of a hurricane.

I remember, years ago, as a medical student having been up all night while on-call. It was one of my very first clinical rotations and I was under the impression I was seriously tired. We were in an antique hospital with fire hoses in glass cases in the corridors, with tall green oxygen tanks chained to the walls. We were walking down an upstairs hall, the intern and myself, turning left then right, then left again, going through hall after hall, through endless corridors, with two-toned walls. Finally, we arrived at a small room on the fifth floor. We poked "our" head inside and saw the senior resident on another service.

He wanted to know what was in the E.R. that might be coming his way.

There was an addict with cellulitis and another man with a left-lower-lobe pneumonia.

(A cellulitis is a skin infection which—in addicts—tends to come from dirty needles).

A pneumonia is a pneumonia.

The resident was unshaven. He had a grey voice. His feet were propped on a desk. I saw the scruffy side of his face.

He did not turn around. He did not flip a page in his journal. What he did was say:

—I love an addict.

That was that. We left. I never saw him again.

In retrospect, I wish I had paid more attention to his face. At this distance, there is something slightly hallucinogenic about the entire episode: the fire hoses seem suspiciously dusty in my mind. I have a feeling that the resident's face may have been my own. But if it *was,* my face, my voice, it was some time before I learned what I meant.

Veins are not just the medium for an addict's salvation but the medium through which a physician must fight what that salvation has done to him. The serious infections that an addict gets can last for weeks and are both deadly and recurrent; which means, for practical purposes, you are never free of your patient. For six weeks, day and night, you will be called repeatedly, paged, beeped: *His I.V. has infiltrated; he has a cellulitis; he has pulled out his central line.* There will come a time when you know every inch of his body. An intravenous line normally takes a few minutes to start. Normally. Not for an addict. Always sleepy, always behind, you will have to search for thirty minutes, for forty minutes, for an hour, for an hour and a half, for one more rush at life. If the problem is endocarditis, a bacterial infection of the heart (which it frequently will be), the course of antibiotics must go for four, five or six weeks and cannot be allowed to stop. As the intern or resident you must keep an access in that body, that *wreck* of a body for six weeks. (Six *weeks.*) When you destroy the veins, you destroy access, for blood, for fluids, for antibiotics, for everything. Finally, you become little more than a spectator, and death the only player that can get on the field.

I remember also (perhaps the same year) a woman in the room with another one of my addicts. She stood aside. His wife? Girlfriend? Frightening what is left of her beauty. How much, I mean. Is she trading sex for drugs? Such a trade, no?

If she would, I would…might anyway. But I am going to collapse right here in front of both of them. It is three in the morning. I am asleep. No I'm not. We wrap his arms in warm towels. I pump up a blood pressure cuff, search for those veins he can't normally reach. For some reason, I saw part of one of the medical student's pharmacology tests today. At what rate must you resume the I.V. to attain an identical blood level of penicillin G if the infusion has stopped for two hours? Was that a joke? I need simpler questions at this time of day. What is my name? How old am I?

Sheepishly, my patient looks at me. Whence this dew of sweat? Why is the woman still standing aside? They are looking at one another. She injected him with something, I know. With a heavy object I could break out the sockets of her eyes. Do whatever you like, but leave my veins alone.

Why do you take care of me, my addict says, does not say, with his eyes. Why do you put up with me? He is sweaty. I am not. I say nothing; there is nothing to say. I don't care for you; the system cares for you; I am trapped by the system. I have been up thirty-eight hours. Only in medicine and the military does one deal with such levels of exhaustion. I care nothing for you, do you hear me? I wish you were dead.

The truth is, Mr. Collan, in the worst of such cases it is difficult to remember when you start pulling against the patient.

—Aren't you going to put on gloves?

We are back in the E.R. now. (Actually, less than forty seconds have passed.) A noise now, an *absence* of noise seems to have distracted me. I am indeed going to put on gloves. For now, with Mr. Collan our G.I. bleeder I must insert a central line.

Ah, here is the tray.

—*Without* epinephrine?

—Yes.

The blue bottle.

(We are referring to the Lidocaine. Did I say that out loud?)

Mr. Collan, if you have a moment, I will show you how to put in a central line. Despite the ham-handed mess people can make of it, it is not that difficult. What is tough, for everyone concerned, are the possible complications.

We need to lay you flat. Almost flat. If we lay you perfectly flat, you can vomit into your lungs. As much as I might like to see you vomit into your lungs, that would be too careless…But wait…Ah…

—Restrain him!

—Get him!

—Mr. Collan!

—Son of a *bitch!*

Mr. Collan is struggling now. He is at least partially in the DT's. Still, I can't sedate him at this pressure. The nurse will have to hold his head down and to one side. She will have to insert her hands underneath the sterile drapes. I noticed they did not specify a race in the ambulance report and now I see why. You seem to be of no race; your skin is not black, not white; not yellow, not red. Your blue snake is all I am truly certain of. Though, come to see more carefully, there is perhaps a *tinge* of yellow in your skin. It may not be real; a mere saffron echo in the light. If it *is* real, I hope this tinge derives from ancestors from some meridian of the tropics, not from bilirubin. I will double-glove for this; if I get AIDS or hepatitis, I want to get it in a more exciting fashion than in your neck. (I find myself looking at the pink bow in the hair of the head nurse.)

What else am I doing, though?

I am feeling the sternal notch in Mr. Collan's neck, and, on either side, the belly of a muscle, the sternocleido-mastoid, a belly forking like a claw; in the crux of that claw, I am going with the point of my needle aiming for the ipsilateral nipple. Good word: ipsi, means same. Ipsi-lateral: same side.

Opposite is contra. Aiming, aiming. Too far to the left, hit the carotid artery; too far to the right, puncture (drop, we call it) the lung. Therefore, I am aiming for the nipple on the same side of the body as the side of the neck I am puncturing. The procedure is slightly easier with males. The nipple stays more put with age.

You ask, isn't there anything more accurate? Or foolproof?

No.

Have you ever hit the carotid? Or the lung?

Have I?

I have no comment on that.

(You hear me, Mr. Collan, I have no comment.)

If I do it tonight, you are dead.

Relax. You may have sensed, and it is true, Mr. Collan, that the thought of killing you has crossed my mind. But I have no intention of killing you through incompetence.

Interesting, as it turns out, the head nurse is holding the head. Should have made a joke about that. Seems a bit late.

We are back in the E.R. now.

—Hold *still* Mr. Collan!

—Tie his feet too.

—He's *pinching* me, dammit!

—Break his fingers.

A warm smile from the nurse that I address this to. *Not* the head nurse. Mr. Collan smiles too; a gold tooth is revealed. There is a moment of lucidity between us all.

—Mr. Collan we are trying to *help* you! Would you please be still!

(Indeed. We may help you more than you dream.)

Observe now, Mr. Collan, I begin with a very narrow needle, a twenty-two gauge, to make sure of my landmarks. If I make a hole in the wrong place, I want it to be a small one. You might as well trust me for the moment, Mr. Collan; I repeat, I am thinking about killing you, but I have no intention of killing you through incompetence. I insert the needle slowly...slowly...but see nothing. I advance some more, pull on the plunger. You are squirming, Mr. Collan; you are making this all the more difficult. Still... nothing...nothing. Then, suddenly, a perfect explosion of blood: turbulent, raw, rosy. I find it impossible to watch it without generating a little sound in my mind, a sort of explosion: ploosh, like a child might make while playing army. Ploosh! I suspect it would be impossible for *you* to watch, Mr. Collan, without a cold chill running down your spine. You and your junkie friends might perhaps try this sometime on a folded blanket in a hallway. Now we go with a much larger needle, a needle with a catheter around it, and do the same thing. There is the blood again. (I look up momentarily and see, midway the table, those tiny testicles of yours. Do you know how that happened? I must tell you later. You must be no slouch of a drinker.) I don't inject the blood back. One of the greatest joys of being a physician is that messes are cleaned up for you. A quarter turn of the syringe unlocks it. What is that, Mr. Collan? No one cleans up messes for you? Except me. I clean up messes for you. You are a mess. I toss the syringe onto a stand. Now the needle comes out. I attach another syringe; recheck, then again. Because the catheter can slip. You really don't want it to slip, Mr. Collan. The blood must shoot— Hold *still* Mr. Collan! The blood must scream out of there. Any trace of a doubt, and I must pull it all out and start over. I must absolutely make myself start over. Am I satisfied? Yes. Yes. You are struggling— *Goddamit! Mr. Collan!* (The head nurse is holding the head.)

The sterile drape is sliding off, falling onto the green tile floor. No matter. Now a guide wire will be placed into the catheter, a wire which will enter your heart. It's OK for the wire to enter your heart, Mr. Collan, it is just not OK for it to go anywhere else. What will be guided by that wire is a sharp plastic sheath, as long as an ice pick and three times the diameter. The sheath will be inserted blindly with only the memory of that plooshing blood of old to guide me. If I am wrong, that sheath is capable of ripping through anything in your body. Now the quide wire is out; the introducer out; the tray a bloody, sharp, dangerous mess. Everything out except one huge catheter with three tubes, called a triple lumen, inside it. Check all of them. Fine, fine. I am not wrong. Everything is fine. OK. Yes.

—I need some two-oh silk…

—It's already on your tray.

Oh.

I pause. Relax. Have time to think. I seem to be more awake. I am sewing a double, then triple throw in the first knot. Now watching big satisfying drops in the clear IV tubing. One each, one liter, of Ringer's lactate and normal saline, running furiously, slowing momentarily, becoming little hurrying globules of light. The wound in your skin is like a tiny mouth where the catheter goes in. The two-oh silk is in my hands. Big silk is such a joy to tie. I pull on your skin like a mattress. Does that hurt, Mr. Collan?

—Did G.I. ever answer?! (I yell, now, to the clerk in her booth while tying another knot).

There is no response. The clerk is behind a fiberglass partition and cannot hear me.

—Ask her if G.I. answered!

—Yes! She says, yes!

—And?

—They're coming!

—Coming?!

(My God.) I seem to be more awake.

—I told them you were busy and couldn't come to the phone!

(My God. My God.)

—Call surgery too! They need to know! If it's arterial it is going to go to them!

(There is no response to this. A silence as I make, complete, the third stitch.)

Why did I say that? Everyone in the room knows it. The truth is, I prefer at all times to say as little medical as possible; it is redundant, silly, flinging jargon and strategies around among nurses and physicians. It is akin to chatting away on a CB Radio (something else I won't do).

—Who's on for surgery?

—Ssss…en gar!

—Who?

—Slazenger!

Ah, the beautiful one. Sleek. Slinky. Very competent too, knows it. Obnoxious as hell. Occasionally wears black stockings and crosses her beautiful ballerina legs while writing orders. My, my. This will be my competition. I am definitely more awake.

Suddenly Mr. Collan vomits. He vomits blood, raw blood. Nothing but blood. He is bleeding again. This is the first bright red blood we have seen from him. There is blood on his chest, his pillow, in his ears. Now filling an emesis basin. He sputters and sputters. There are red bubbles everywhere. He is bleeding again. (Though, in truth, we tend not to phrase it that way. What we tend to say is that he has broken open.) You're going to love what comes next, Mr. Collan, I might have refrained. Oh boy.

Without waiting for an order, the nurse begins to tear open a large plastic bag with a clear plastic tube inside. From the yellow container I begin spraying Cetacaine in the back of Mr. Collan's throat to numb it slightly.

Sorry, Mr. Collan, we have to lavage you. (Mr. Collan is gagging now.) Does that hurt? I'm afraid the pain is very specifically *your* problem. You are bleeding because of your endless years of drinking. How many times have you been told to cut the drinking out? How many times have you sneered at us? You and your cohorts have beat us to death, day and night, with your sclerosed and collapsed veins, with your overdoses, your DT's and episodes of pancreatitis. You are not completely disoriented at the moment; you, are beginning to see what we have seen from the very first, that you may die right here, right now. This recognition on your part indeed gives some satisfaction. The terror in your eyes gives some satisfaction. You are the little bully, the tow-headed unmanageable brat who has at last stuck his finger in the fan. The first emotion we must all deal with is a sort of glee.

There is blood everywhere now. This is not good. I attach a fifty c.c. catheter-tipped syringe full of water to the Ewald and inject it into your stomach.

Your mouth is around the clear, plastic Ewald tube, something like a fish on a stringer.

What I pull back is raw blood. (And more blood. And more blood.)

In a movie or on TV the sound track would get louder at this moment to indicate anxiety. But any anxiety we feel is, in fact, very superficial; the truth is the blood has a calming effect; there is no longer the slightest doubt of what needs to be done. Indeed, for my part, Mr. Collan, I suspect I could watch you die as dispassionately as I could watch water boil. It is a paradox, really; if I stay in this mood, I will do a better job. There is no chance of my fumbling or dropping anything, no chance of my missing a vein. You may benefit enormously if I stay in this mood.

I become like the gambler who cannot lose.

Again and again, filling the syringe with water, clear, cold, not sterile, but nevertheless pure; again and again, injecting it down the Ewald into Mr. Collan's stomach; again and again pulling back the same water once more, newly full of swirling blood and clots. Then discarding that water.

Mr. Collan may wonder why we aren't doing anything else. (I am not at all certain I am as awake as I think I am.) What Mr. Collan is looking for is a little plastic bag of blood for us to hang up and run into him. In truth *we* are looking for a bag of blood, but know it can't arrive yet. Still, we have done something in addition to the fluid and lavage. We have started a clock in our minds. Mr. Collan thinks he is one big skein, one limitless bladder of blood. He is not. He is only about six quarts, only some five thousand five hundred tiny little cubic centimeters of blood. He is a not so big a bladder of blood. He is a bladder it is not so difficult to empty.

With the onset of the bleeding, we have a moment to ourselves. Another paradox, perhaps. Mr. Collan seems to be watching me now. Perhaps he is wondering how I plan to kill him, especially in such a small room, with so many witnesses. Patience, my friend. You won't see. More correctly, you won't understand. For that matter, no one in this room is going to see or understand.

Allow me to give you an analogy:

Imagine, please, a chess master who has decided always to make only the most obvious move. He would be defeated and quickly, but his defeat would have little or nothing to do with his opponent. He would be defeated by the nature of the game.

I want to defeat you by the nature of the game.

(With each syringe, we are adding, counting: pink, red, pink, pink, pink, pink.)

The housekeeper is in the room now. The housekeeper with his mop is mopping. The housekeeper with his mop is adding as well. He is not adding quite the same way we are. (So difficult to remember when my mind was not encumbered with anatomy.) But even the housekeeper knows, what he sees on the sheets, on the floor, on our yellow gloves and smeared onto the chrome of the stretcher, is a lot. *This*...is a lot. So much in. So much out. Anyone will begin to add, to start a little clock running in their minds. Mr. Collan too, no doubt, is adding. Mr. Collan is not adding quite the same way we are. Mr. Collan has grown accustomed to being alive.

What I see this time in the barrel of the syringe is not nearly so red. Only pink. The next time, too, only pink. A deeper pink. What we are really dealing with here is time, not necessarily hours. Add for pink. Subtract for red.

Beep. (Blood pressure.) Sixty-eight over twenty: 68/20. Oh boy.

A nurse has the computer printout of his history.

—Do you want to hear it?

(Did I answer? I don't think I did.)

—There are three admissions for DT's. One...two...three for pancreatitis, one for pancreatic pseudocyst, two for cellulitis...alcoholic cardiomyopathy. Three for reactive depression. One for cocaine abuse. Three for overdoses. One for substance abuse, unspecified. One for rule-out endocarditis...

—Did it rule out?

(I am liking the idea of killing you more and more, Mr. Collan.)

—No... Yes! Yes it did!

—How about hepatitis?

—No.

—AIDS?!

—No.

—Do you see any problem that is *not* drug or alcohol related?

—No... Correction! One! Merely a problem, though, not an admission: an ingrown toenail.

—Ah.

My complete abuser. I love you. Please don't die on me before I can rip your soul out. I can imagine your saying, years ago, in a bar somewhere, while raising a heavy glass, how you would rather *die* than do without this stuff. Excellent! I hope you remember that. This is *the* room for forgotten promises. (We also answer rhetorical questions.) But there are larger things.

Goddamit!

(I look up and see a nursing assistant shaking her hand vigorously.)

—He pinched the *hell* out of me!

—Did he break the skin?

—No.

—Good.

(No paperwork.)

Sorry, Mr. Collan. As I said, larger things: concerning the drugs, not the ones you took but the one you injected in your veins. Something happened there, didn't it? Something you did not expect, something you were never able to forget. You woke them up. You became like a puppet grown aware of its strings; hung-up, gazing, mouth not quite awry. Your veins started feeling empty. You became *aware* of the interior of your vasculature. It became vaguely itchy, alternately thin and congested, sometimes like a golden chain dangling in the hollow of the your body, sometimes like the clapper for a bell. Your veins were asleep and you woke them up and now they won't lie dormant again. Your veins were *asleep!* (I tell you) and you woke them up forever.

How do I know this?

Don't ask how I know it.

—Surgery wants to know if you can come to the phone!

(A voice, suddenly, from the clerk, from behind the screen.)

Can I come to the phone?

The clerk cannot see me. It makes little sense, really, what I say next:

—Does it *look* like I can come to the phone!

This is an arterial bleed. Must be. (But one truly cannot tell.)

The clerk enters the room. More quietly she relays the message: The surgeon says to stabilize him and she will be here in a few minutes.

Tell the beautiful, competent but obnoxious surgeon that this man is not *going* to stabilize.

(This is what I think. But I say nothing, merely nod. The surgeon will be down soon.)

Wonderful. Actually, I very much like the sound of what the clerk has just said. Surgery says *she*. Surgery is feminine tonight. Like the fates, the muses. Like what else? Like Eve. Like ships at sea. But this *man*. If you call this a man. Look at him. I wonder whether junkies are made in the image of God. No? Yes? Perhaps?

It's an image I do not like, evidently.

I remember one addict, a nice guy, truly. He was taking a correspondence course in air-conditioner repair. Very proud of how well he was doing. I wanted very much for him never to be embarrassed at his pride. I made an attempt to hide my fairly considerable education while in the room with him. I left it at the door, hid it at the end of the hall, sat on the opposite bed and talked with him. We talked of three-phase motors and rotary compressors. (What do I know of three-phase motors and rotary compressors? Plenty, actually.) He had kicked, was more or less cured, was even losing that anxious and faraway look of a man not making it in life. But I made it clear:

You do the drugs again, you die.

Yes, yes.

Big problem though: girlfriend junkie.

He was back two weeks later. Temperature 102. Pulse 128. (Pressure 96/50.)

Why you do this?

Love.

It was love that devastated his heart. Very soon thereafter, bacteria like tiny claws began snagging out his valves. We knew he might stroke any second. (He did stroke, later.) Despite enormous, *mega* doses we call them, of antibiotics, despite preparations for immediate surgery, the bacteria and fibrin and antibodies got ahead of us, began ripping out the valves of his heart, sludging vegetations and plaques. Tricuspid going. Mitral, going. Aortic going, going, going, going… Bits and pieces of bacteria and platelets and heart drifting off into blood stream. Love will be triumphant! The emboli can go anywhere now, like sparks from a fire. Exactly like sparks. A showering of emboli. Little sparks, perhaps no problem. (At least *maybe* no problem.) Big sparks. Fire! Always fire! Fire in kidneys! Fire in brain! Brain like a dandelion. Paralyzed perhaps. Can hit anywhere! Suddenly. Completely unpredictable. Can no longer use little finger; can no longer use left foot; can no longer see. Entire left side of body gone. From second-to-second and minute-to-minute it keeps happening and may not stop. Love will be triumphant! The devastation is not over soon like in regular stroke. It keeps happening. Thirty-six years old. Sure could have used left side of body a little longer. With these air conditioners and heavy rotary compressors, had real use for left side of body.

—*Doctor!*

Well. Well. In truth, we are seldom so formal. (Doctor, indeed.) Was I asleep? No. But according to the cardiac monitor, Mr. Collan is now in V tach. This is an inherently formal rhythm. Ventricular tachycardia. It looks like a sine wave. The heart is galloping too fast to fill with blood. V tach is a very elegant-appearing rhythm if one can get over what it means. (One can never quite get over what it means.) It means the patient has minutes, sometimes seconds to live. Most humans cannot pump blood at this rate. Some can. Most cannot. Mr. Collan cannot. I know very well he cannot. Mr. Collan's eyes are rolling back in his head. We get very formal now. Now is not the time to kill him. Everyone knows exactly what needs to be done. Aesthetically, I very much like the look of V tach. Though, in truth, it's not my favorite waveform. Torsades-de-pointes is my favorite. It shows what complex forces are driving the world. Torsades is equally deadly. More so.

A commotion sure enough now. Open the crash cart. Go for the defibrillator. Cables too short. Unlock the stretcher. I am wide, wide awake, of a sudden. Unlock the stretcher and pull it out. We are going to have a forty-five second delay. I'm going to try to tube him while he's down. Seconds. Seconds, we have.

What has happened here? It is the old tale of muscle and nerve, embryologically elaborate variations on a theme. Vectors and impedances. Buddies. Sometimes look out for one another, sometimes argue. Buddies, I say, brothers too, especially in the heart, fight, though, on occasion, especially in moments of great stress. When the fight gets out of hand, a third party may yell *Doctor!* and point out a beautiful sine wave on a monitor.

—I need a laryngoscope and a number eight tube! And the Yankauer suction!

(I would not do this first if I could get to the defibrillator immediately. Can't. So.)

When I finish putting in the tube, what we are going to have to do is stop the heart. When we do this, especially in this situation, it may not start again. Possible. Happens. Sometimes yes. Sometimes no. If it does not start again, we (I) will pronounce the patient dead. I am completely dispassionate. I am also the gambler who cannot lose. I look at the monitor. V tach, still. What will be next? V fib. Then asystole.

Yes. Next will be asystole.

Would you like to know a little more about it?

Imagine a cemetery. Sunny day. Imagine exhuming a body buried for ten years. Pry open the casket. Spill the body out onto the warm close-cut cemetery grass. Undress the body. Ignore any mold. Ignore any changes in features. Ignore the heavily sutured and unhealed cuts from the embalming trochars. Ignore anything and everything that would suggest that it has not been exactly *pleasant* to have been dead for ten years. Attach an EKG machine. Turn the machine on. The rhythm displayed on the screen will be asystole. It is a rhythm for all time.

But now. Yankauer suction. 10 cc syringe. Copper stylet. I am rather good at this. Thank God I am good at this; this would be a terrible thing to be bad at. Laryngoscope, tongue, throat, blood everywhere. Suction, suction. A feeling of literally tunneling into the body. The narrow, grey, corrugated look of the trachea. There! Easy. Good. Clear. Clot like a leech, dangling from the tip of the suction.

Nothing to be too proud of here, intubation easy, very easy in this guy. (I stand up. Memories of loose skin, tucked like an upholsterer into the forbidden orifices of the body.)

Am I pulling against myself? No. This man must *not* die naturally.

On the monitor I see Mr. Collan has slipped into V fib. Formal name: ventricular fibrillation. A certain *species* of lay person who is always cruising at the limits of his knowledge will use that name, too. (Is she in ventricular fibrillation, doctor?) Otherwise, it would never be said. Vee Tach, Vee Fib, we would say. Then we would say: asystole. The head nurse has the paddles ready, is passing them over, setting the controls.

—How much?

—Two hundred.

Joules, I mean.

Named after James Prescott Joule who discovered the mechanical equivalent of heat. There is an electrical equivalent, too. We shall fire it like a lightning bolt through this man's body. It is enough to weld small pieces of metal together. *Joules* equals work: power integrated over time; 20,000 volts over a small fraction of a second. With this we will depolarize each and every cell of the heart simultaneously, in a way they have never been depolarized. This will stop the heart. There will be a moment of pure and utter silence that has not been present in Mr. Collan's body since many months before birth. One can imagine the heart saying to itself, "What?"

Then, hopefully, starting again in a better-behaved fashion.

It doesn't *have* to start again. Ever. Regardless of chest compression, epinephrine, atropine. If it doesn't, we (I) shall fill out a death certificate. We (I) shall use black ink.

—Synchronized?

She knows the answer to this, but must ask.

(Evidently I answered. I don't *remember* answering, actually.) Everyone away from the stretcher now.

Ka BAM!

In truth there can't be such a noise. Why does there always seem to be such a noise? What *is* there to make a noise? What there mainly is is a lot of motion. The patient is liable to buck vertically off the bed. It's an opisthotonic sort of bucking. In Michelangelo's Sistine-Chapel portrait of the damned-in-hell, he shows an opisthotonic sort of writhing. It's the same here. It always seems to occur in slow motion, too, a slow curling motion, a gyrating spasm with slow release. Orgasm?

Eyes on monitor. Eyes glued to monitor. Nothing nothing. There. Oops. No: Vee Fib. The defibrillation did not work. Vee fib again.

(Mr. Collan's conjunctiva are beginning to look like the fairy wings on the surface of milk.)

This is it.

Everyone must get away from the stretcher. Plenty of energy in this little machine. Plenty of energy to stop more than one heart forever. Like a gigantic orgasm? Possibly. Doesn't *feel* like an orgasm, evidently. This is not going to work.

—360 joules!

[I have a collection, a small one, very small (two patients) of what people have said after being resurrected from this quiver of the heart. Eyes rolled back, essentially dead. Then Ka BAM! Most say nothing, too knocked out. But two did, immediately. A small series, the words of the dead. What do dead men say?]

One said:

—Son of a *bitch!*

The other said:

—You do that again and I'll *kill* you!

But Mr. Collan is going to say nothing. Mr. Collan has a tube down his throat.

—Three-sixty! (I say again.)

We are set at three hundred and sixty. Prescott Joule would be proud.

—Now! Clear! Go. *Clear!*

Ka BAM!

Eyes glued on the monitor. Nothing. Nothing. Then: a pulse. Another. A sinus pulse. (Good P wave.) Sinus brady. Full sinus. My God! Well, well, well. Sinus rhythm. Going faster now. Sinus tach. Sinus anyway. Good enough. *Feel* a pulse with it too. Good pulse. A successful defibrillation.

Must move quickly now.

Now that he is intubated, we shall place him in Trendelenburg: feet high, head low to improve his blood pressure. Good. Good… Suction. Good. A miracle. Nothing down there. Afraid he might have vomited into the lungs. He didn't. But he is exhausted. He will collapse for a while. We are breathing for him externally now, fluid and blood are external too. Tubes, tubes everywhere, even in his bladder. Aspects of his body are becoming peripheral.

The clerk is approaching the stretcher. She evidently has a message for me. What is going on?

—It's surgery again. She wants to know…

—What do you *mean* she wants to know? Where *is* she?

(*She* is the one who was supposed to save him. Not I.)

The clerk seems as fascinated as we are by this blue tattooed snake.

—The surgeon wants to know if you can come to the phone.

—Does it *look* like I can come to the phone? Tell her to get her ass down here!

I simply cannot believe that it converted.

A bit of giggling now, among my team.

(We are in Trendelenburg and sinus rhythm after all.)

I look at what is coming out of the Ewald. It is pink. But only slightly. Almost clear. Incredible. I wonder if shocking him had any effect? Vaguely possible perhaps; platelet aggregation is at least partially electrical, something like that, very interesting. Can't be, though, probably just a coincidence or the Pitressin may be having an effect. Merely light pink. Pure coincidence, I am sure.

Completely out of it now, curled up, Mr. Collan has begun trying to bite me. But he can't because of the Ewald and ET tubes. From a creature of need, he has become a bundle of reflexes. *Where* is the blood?

You're exhausting me, Mr. Collan.

I am now breathing for you, squeezing the Ambu bag. I have taken over the most primitive of reflexes. So here, you see, Mr. Collan, I have made the most menial task my own. I could easily delegate this. But I can run things from here as well as anywhere. In fact, I enjoy breathing for you.

The conventional wisdom is that drugs are an escape from reality. In truth, I do not see them that way. Take you, Mr. Collan; you are largely with us. You are largely intact. Only your veins are gone. Things can and probably will get much worse. I see the apocryphal addict: now a diabetic because his pancreas has been destroyed; now a dialysis patient because his kidneys have been fried; now breathless because his heart has failed. Finally there is only one thing left: Or is there? The apocryphal addict, elbowing his way across the desert of his physiology, has no will whatsoever. He is a creature of needs alone. In fact, he has become a most primitive animal.

(Very early, the young physician learns about drug-seeking patients. They talk only and always of the pain, the pain, the *pain*! Then one day he understands.)

They are talking about something outside of their bodies.

Beep:
94 over 48.

A much better bottom number on the blood pressure...

.Where *is* the blood? My, my, how slow it can be. Five, ten, fifteen or twenty minutes. Twenty minutes is a long time to ignore eyes that are dying. Still, Mr. Collan is doing better. Spoke too soon. Spoke too soon.

(Didn't speak at all, actually.) He is vomiting raw blood again.

This man is going to die.

No, I do not, cannot, see drugs as an escape, but as moving toward something very central and primitive: a beginning, if you like, a primordial swamp or Garden of Eden. One can define reality variously, and repeatedly because it is repeatedly various. Reality is peripheral, an accident. But for the abusers there is a center, a common ground.

Mr Collan, we intersect you in your progress toward that common ground.

There are more people in the room now. A domino effect. As a bleed proceeds, through a process I have never quite understood, there is a gathering of unfamiliar faces. I am nominally in charge and yet this happens. Even in a hospital, a G.I. bleed is something that happens where it happens and tends to be treated where it happens. There is not a lot of moving the patient about. Such a bleed is very often the terminal event. Any place seems good enough to die.

Case in point. Observe: medical students. We seldom see medical students in the E.R. They are not required to be here, so they don't come. Medical students can hide in a hole a rat couldn't crawl into. They have heard a rumor, perhaps. One of the students is watching as the blood is swabbed and smeared with a thick mop on the floor. There is a faint water-color wash being left on the tiles. Medical students have begun to see what they are in for, what this profession is all about that they have entered. They become desperate to protect their last years of freedom. Two students here now: one male, one female. No three: two males, one female. Where did they come from? Who are they? Where are they going? Poor little happy things.

—What's his pressure?
What?
(Suddenly, here, at last, we have a new voice.)
At last, here, suddenly, we have the surgeon, somewhat breathless, in fact. (My God what a doll.) Truly, I thought I remembered her face, but it seems I had forgotten the details. I can scarcely look directly at her. I *can't* look directly at her. One should not look so fine in scrubs. Her face and hands appear raw they are so freshly scrubbed. Her ears are set close to her head like a model. Every one of my crew, rather striking women themselves, notices her. This surgeon looks like an advertisement for something.
Life on earth, perhaps.
—What's his pressure? she repeats.
(A physician after my own heart.)
But I wonder myself, now.
103/56.
(My God.)
—Is G.I. coming?
—They're here. *He's* here. I saw him pass.
I wonder what the clerk said. I repeat the story to the surgeon: I tell her I think it may be arterial. It may *be* arterial. Still, I wonder what the clerk said.
My nurses are almost glaring at her. The head nurse is retaping a recently established IV site. The head nurse establishes eye contact with me, a look I cannot begin to interpret. My God, how complex this is becoming. The beautiful female surgeon as dominatrix. We should dwell on this at some later time.
Mr. Collan is still vomiting but the vomitus is less red now. Sometimes even severe bleeds suddenly stop. (This one is not going to stop.) Of course, you can never know.

But this one is not going to stop. Blue pads on the floor now to keep us from slipping.

Running fluid into his veins, his own blood slushed with it though his heart, then out through stomach and Ewald; onto the bed, in bedpans, in cracks in the stretcher, in the joints of the stretcher, in bloody feces and on the floor and walls. I see some blood on a Mayo stand. In great explosive eruptions, the blood may go so far as to hit the ceiling. We have had one or two such eruptions already. I look up, curiously, then see it, fresh, it seems; two or three drops, no more: a duality, trinity, of sorts.

I look very shallowly into his eyes.

Beep. Pressure is… Never mind what the pressure is. But good. Good. OK, at least.

Do you know how long ten or fifteen minutes are in this situation?

Wait. Wait. Wait.

How slow it all is: Wait, wait, wait, wait, wait, wait wait, wait wait…

(The surgeon is reading through the chart.)

I glance back at Mr. Collan. Funny: his eyes are very alert now. He knows he is dying. He sees a lot of work going on around him. He is the focus for a lot of work, perfectly meaningless to him: instruments, tubes, monitors. He is wondering, waiting, fearing perhaps. What is it going to be like to die? There is a pleasure, truly, in observing this.

I look up at the cardiac monitor, the green tracings on the scope. Good P wave. Good QRS. (Pronounced as individual letters: Q…R…S…) Rate of 120. OK… What can I say? OK.

Mr. Collan seems to be watching me now, watching my hands on the Ambu bag, watching other things, wondering what I am thinking. In truth I wonder what *you* are thinking, Mr. Collan. I sense you are accusing me of being coarse, or blasphemous. Blasphemous! Please, my friend! Do be civil… *Blasphemous!* Don't make me laugh.

Don't you see what the real problem is, at this moment, between God and myself?

We both want to kill you, Mr. Collan.

Maybe this woman can stop us. This woman indeed. Would you please look at this woman. I seem to love all the orifices of the female body, especially the one I almost can't get to: the cervix, the little entrance to the womb, like the nose of a puppy on a rubbery fruit. The Bible got it wrong, if one can say such a thing meaningfully: women, knowledge, sin, life, death, good and evil; the symbol should not be an apple; it should be a pear. The womb does not *feel* like an apple; it feels like a pear, like a rubbery fruit.

I glance now at the surgeon still reading through Mr. Collan's chart, her ballerina legs crossed, a golden chain with golden links dangling from her left wrist.

Now, here, at last, the bags of blood arrive. Two at once, in fact. We shall hang one bag, wait a few minutes, then hang the other. (I think, but say nothing.)

Meanwhile the nurse has already snagged the first bag on the IV pole. Without asking me, I mean. Am I in charge here or not? Probably not. What would she have done had I said no?

But you have a prayer now, Mr. Collan.

I squeeze the Ambu to give you oxygen and air. The large plastic bag resembles a huge olive. The bag is red with blood. The blood doesn't stick to the plastic, doesn't coat it, I mean. Very interesting. Blood soaks into cotton and wool, drifts into water, doesn't quite seem to know what to do in the face of plastic.

I am coasting at the moment, rambling perhaps; a physician is fundamentally *about* decisions and there are no decisions to be made just now. Activity has become a blur in the room around me. I am responsible for *you*, Mr. Collan, not the activity. G.I. is here now. I see the gastroscope being assembled. When the gastroenterologist arrived, we looked at each other and laughed. My crew looks like a bunch of kids who have had a blood fight. I suppose there is no such thing as a blood fight, but if there is, we have had it.

(I see the fiber-optic scope, black, snake-like. I pull the Ewald out to allow room for the scope.)

The surgeon is now on the phone, now looking at the lab slips. I am still pumping the Ambu. Why? Because there is no room for a ventilator anymore. And because I find it mindless and relaxing.

But the surgeon I cannot ignore. Would you please look at this woman. I saw her once at a party for the residents in fishnet stockings and a short skirt. I really could not quite believe what I saw. Why don't we step over here, mademoiselle, my dear and glorious physician? This is what women are for, you know, for starting over. With your aid, in one bed, merely a stretcher if you like, we could start a new set of veins, a new liver, new fresh skin, fresh clear eyes, something very like or called hope. This *man* has some fundamental problems now. With the aid of your body we could start anew. You are cocky about your brilliance and dexterity, but everything in your brain or mine is as nothing compared to what your uterus knows. We could expand that rubbery fruit of yours, cause it to grow. Your body is wise, no doubt; I would like to feel its wisdom. No, actually, I would not. It is late; I am tired, tired past exhaustion, rambling now, virtually incoherent. I want nothing quite so esoteric.

I want to crawl into your vagina and let my ankles dangle out.

We are a crowd now: a horde. There is a problem with the light for the scope. No, it's OK. The fuse was blown. Can't believe there was another fuse. The surgeon with her perfect hands is palpating Mr. Collan's abdomen. Mr. Collan seems to be bleeding more now. I watch G.I. with his scope peering, like a voyeur, deep into the depths of the body, twisting, turning. It is all in the wrist. Then:

—It's arterial, he says, definitely arterial. Near the duodenum.

Do I want to look?

No.

Actually, I want to continue looking at the hands of the surgeon.

Am I losing track? Part of me seems to be alone in this room. I have withdrawn mentally. My presence is not particularly needed anymore. I see G.I., the fiber-optic scope being removed, the brilliant tip like a blue-white star. Perhaps we can have a little less of the vasopressors. Where are we on the Dopamine? 15 mikes. We could go to ten, maybe. No, maybe not. Maybe we should hold what we've got. Fifteen is OK.

Mr. Collan has opened up more now. He has opened up significantly more. He will never last till everyone arrives.

I feel the stretcher being unlocked. I feel the stretcher actually moving. What's happening? Did I miss something? Did I fall asleep?

I look at the head nurse:

—They are moving him *now*? I say.

—They are thinking about a Swan.

—Let them think about it in the SICU.

—They're not *going* to the SICU. They are going directly to the O.R.

—What about the *team*?

—The team is already here.

What!??

(A silence in my mind. Let me count, one, two, three, all the meaningless seconds of silence in my mind. *How?* Why? It's past midnight.)

—There's a perfed cecum in room seven, she says.

Oh.

Ah, so. A perforated cecum; a patient's abdomen is full of feces. As a consequence, the team is here; the entire operating team is here; now, upstairs, as we speak, cutting, cleansing, resecting, wearing their pale gloves, using their shiny silver forceps like chopsticks. The scrub nurses, the anesthesiologist, the chief surgical resident, a staff attending, all are here, now, ready for *you* next, Mr. Collan.

(One man's feces is another man's luck.)

My God! Look at you, eyes awake, so alert again. I had not noticed that. Something else I had not noticed. But we won't speak of that.

Despite all effort, it is still going to be a coin toss for you. Beep: Pressure is holding, too. 94/48.

They need to untangle some IV tubing to get the stretcher out. We have one final moment, you and I. You look so alert. But your eyes are scared, wondering, looking around. The stretcher is moving. Where are you now? Where are you going? Let me explain:

You are in the valley of the shadow of death.

I wonder whether it is wise for you to leave it. Bleeds are very messy to look at, but a good death otherwise, and rather painless. You were already delirious; the worst was over for you. You may have been heading toward a golden sunrise (a *vision* I saw, I think). At least you were until we got in your way. It is not my fault, you know; I had other plans, or think I did. *Maybe* I did. Who knows? I've had other plans innumerable times before and never acted on them.

It's a means of staying awake.

*   *   *

An hour and a half later, the calm has returned. Everyone is gone. The E.R. has been completely cleaned, except for a few dots of blood which are drying still on the ceiling. There is a vague hum of machinery. One might imagine the Titanic having missed the iceberg. Then suddenly, unexpectedly, a messenger arrives, very literally, a man from a messenger service. He is carrying a little Styrofoam cooler of B-negative blood which is being relayed from another hospital. I can imagine the messenger himself an hour previously, in a room with a telephone, a TV, a toaster, some Pop-Tarts. Blood is needed immediately! Carry this blood! The voyeur in him thinks there might be some excitement at the other end. He arrives, like an embarrassed guest, apologetic with his gift. But sees nothing, Nothing, only our empty stretchers, our green and spotless tiles. Nothing happening here either; the party is elsewhere now. He is disappointed, has disappointment in his eyes. World everywhere the same.

We direct the messenger appropriately, then talk among ourselves.

—You think he's still alive?

—Maybe.

(Not only do we not know, we cannot even guess.)

When the messenger returns and is on his way out, we ask him:

—Is he still alive?

—They didn't say anything. They took the blood, though.

—They would take it either way, I say. I glance at my watch. It's too early to call upstairs. We will call later. I am not sure I want to know at this moment. The truth is (as you perhaps have realized by now) Mr. Collan's face, like that of my resident of long ago, was not totally unfamiliar to me.

Soon afterward, an aide asks.

—Whose nail file is this?

—Nail file?

—The fingernail file here on the desk.

(The aide picks it up and we pause, all of us, to look at it.)

—Maybe the medical student left it as a plant, the head nurse says.

—As a *plant*? I say.

—As a plant. As an excuse to come back and talk to you later.

—Why would she want to do that? I say.

THE PUPPIES

Some months ago, my mother's dog Kayceil (pronounced kay-seal) had seven puppies. Two were still-born with cranial defects, and were buried immediately. Two more, the only males, both the runt and the largest of the litter— and both perfect in form—lived a bit more than a day, then, somewhat mysteriously, stopped breathing and died and were removed from the company of their tiny sisters. My mother placed them in a little stainless-steel pan and put the pan in the freezing-compartment of the refrigerator, where, as far as I know, they remain to this day, nestled together, curled and frosty.

She says she talks to them every time she opens that compartment.

The following is their story:

It was within us. It was there. It was in our hearts and lungs. The air and blood and the life, like in every living thing, we had it. But it slipped away, too fast for telling.

Like every thing that ever lived, it was there inside us. We felt it but there was nothing to hold to, no way to grab. And we lost it before we saw each other's face.

We heard for weeks and months the voices in our blood that spoke of things that were to be: cats, rabbits, birds, rocks, trees and sand. And everything the voices said about them. But the voices didn't say what they would *look* like.

You will know them when you see them they said. You will know them when you smell them. Don't worry about the shapes. You will know. And you will understand.

Exactly what Life was they did not explain.

Or exactly how we would recognize it.

What the voices were very clear about, though, was that you had to be sure you were ready, because there was no correcting of mistakes after you were born.

My big brother and I would talk about what we were going to do when we were dogs:

When we are dogs, I said, if we are chasing a rhinoceros...

A rhinoceros is not one of the animals we're supposed to *chase*! You haven't been paying attention to the voices.

I have too.

A rhinoceros is too *big*!

Maybe we'll be big *dogs*!

Even big dogs don't chase rhinoceroses!

You don't know. If we're chasing a rhinoceros, what we'll do is chase it in a big circle and I'll stop and hide behind a rock and then we'll meet again and head it off together!

You haven't been listening to the voices at *all*!

I have too! I don't see why we can't chase a rhinoceros if we want to. We're going to be *dogs*!

Let's not argue.

Let's not.

We'll see.

We'll see.

Our mother can tell us.

That's right.

Still, I don't see why we can't chase a rhinoceros if we want to...

We would always remind each other that our very first job would be to look for life. There will have to be a trail, my brother said. We've got to get on the trail. We'll be the first on it! We'll get on it before the girls! They don't know *any*thing!

But the voices never said where it would be.

Then there was the night when, like electricity, it went through us all. We are going to be born!

We knew.

Tomorrow.

We were so confined. But that night, so excited. We heard more about grass and trees. And excitement peeping through. We'll run, run, run, when we're born. We will be brothers! We're going to be *dogs!* Just your nose under.

But that night the membrane I was in broke.

Will I need it? I said. It broke. I didn't break it. It broke, I said. Will that be OK?

Later my big brother asked the voices.

My little brother broke his membrane, will he need it?

I didn't break it. It broke, I said.

There was no answer.

The voices speak but don't answer.

There will be a forgetting of this time, they said. A forgetting.

We're ready to forget!

But, at times, a dim remembering...

We're ready to remember, too!

We're going to get on the *trail!*

Then we were out.

It felt so big! It was dark, like they said, but immediately we felt the milk. We knew. The voices were right. My brother was next to me. We were the first ones out. We were on the trail! There will be a forgetting of this time too, they had said.

I was so worried about my membrane. But now I saw it didn't matter. It would have broken anyway. Mine just broke a little early is all. Everything was going to be OK. I was so glad. I had worried all night long about my membrane.

The voices had told us all about breathing but they hadn't told us what it would *feel* like. With breathing in you could feel yourself go up slightly. And breathing out was down. So strange. Up, down. Gently.

Up, down. Up, down with the breathing. So very strange. We're going to be *dogs*. No, no, no. Listen to me, talking. We *are* dogs. We're dogs *now*!

But then something began to happen. When I went down, it seemed I did not come up again quite as far. I would go down on one breath, and up not quite as far on the next. I had to remember, too. I had to remember a lot. My brother also noticed it. But he thought something was stuck in his throat. He began to cough and cough to try to get it out. We've got to get on the *trail* he said!

Breathing in was coming up. Breathing out was going down. It was like a balance. But I kept going slightly more down than up. Down and down. I got so I couldn't remember exactly how to get up again. I was forgetting how to breathe! I was so scared. I was doing it *wrong!* Wait. Wait. Help, I said.

Suddenly I was all alone. It was so cold. I was so scared. I've never been so scared. But a dog is supposed to be brave. Almost as suddenly, though, it was all OK. Everything was OK because my brother was with me and we were snuggled together. What had happened, though? Where had our mother gone? And what about the milk?

Then I heard my brother. He had just realized something. You *can't* find life, he said. There's no trail; the trail goes nowhere. It was within us. They didn't tell us where to *look*. But I can see now; it was *within* us. Who would have guessed? Who would have possibly guessed?

I would, I said. You didn't ask *me*.

It was within us. Who would have guessed?

I would. I would have guessed. Even a rhinoceros would have guessed *that*.